Kickin' It at the Dojo . . .

Joe and I stood helpless as Trudy cut through the brown tape sealing the box. We looked at each other, panicked.

"There you go." Aunt Trudy stepped back, leaving us to unpack our own disaster. "Did you get what you wanted?"

We had no choice. Slowly I reached out and opened the top flaps of the box. *Please let it be something innocent looking,* I thought.

I glanced down and saw two black karate outfits with white belts.

I don't know what I was expecting, but not this. As I lifted the uniforms from the box, Joe reached in and pulled out a karate book and a martial-arts-themed video game. Other karate gear had been packed in under the book—exercise mats for falling and sparring gloves.

"Yeah, Aunt Trudy, this is pretty much what we ordered. It's, um . . . karate stuff," I finished, hoping there would be no further inquiry.

"I can see that. But why?" Aunt Trudy never backed down easily.

"Actually, Trudy, this is my doing," Dad said, coming into the kitchen just in time. "The boys mentioned they were interested in learning more about martial arts, so I ordered them th

THE HARDY BOYS
UNDERCOVER BROTHERS™

Available from Simon & Schuster

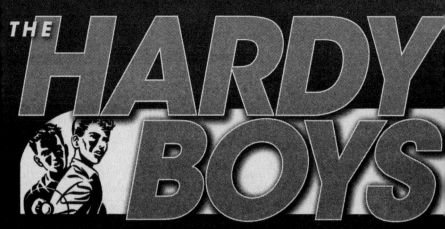

THE HARDY BOYS

UNDERCOVER BROTHERS

#9 Martial Law

FRANKLIN W. DIXON

Aladdin Paperbacks
New York   London   Toronto   Sydney

◆ ALADDIN PAPERBACKS
An imprint of Simon & Schuster
Children's Publishing Division
1230 Avenue of the Americas
New York, NY 10020

Copyright © 2006 by Simon & Schuster, Inc.

THE HARDY BOYS MYSTERY STORIES and HARDY BOYS
UNDERCOVER BROTHERS are trademarks of Simon & Schuster, Inc.
ALADDIN PAPERBACKS and colophon are trademarks of
Simon & Schuster, Inc.
Designed by Lisa Vega
The text of this book was set in Aldine 401BT.
Manufactured in the United States of America
First Aladdin Paperbacks edition April 2006
10 9 8 7

Library of Congress Control Number: 2005929899
ISBN-13: 978-1-4169-0398-7
ISBN-10: 1-4169-0398-4

TABLE OF CONTENTS

1

Racing Waves

"Whoo-hoo!" I screamed above the roar of my engine.

Catching some serious air on a Jet Ski always makes me want to yell. It was a perfect spring day out on the water. Blue skies, blue ocean—great for showing off and splashing down.

My Jet Ski touched down to one side of the speedboat's wake. I glanced over my shoulder at my older brother, Frank. He was on a Jet Ski too. You'd think he would be as psyched as me, but he didn't look ready to whoop it up. Instead he gave me the patented Frank Hardy "get serious" glare and motioned with his hand for me to pull up on the opposite side of the boat.

That's Frank in a nutshell—all business. He has

1

no appreciation for a good moment. Sure, we were out on the open seas chasing down a criminal on a case for ATAC, American Teens Against Crime. Sure, E. J. Kingdon, the lowlife we were after this time, had a gun and had already made it clear he wasn't afraid to use it. And sure, we were racing far enough out to sea that soon our Jet Skis wouldn't be able to take us all the way back to shore.

But we'd been in worse shape than this before. That's what we do—face life-threatening situations and have a seriously great time doing it. Oh, and take down the bad guys.

And E. J. was a genuinely bad guy. Posing as a friendly janitor, he'd stolen explosives and other bomb-making materials from a local college laboratory. ATAC got wind of it and sent us in as eager high school students getting a jump on the college search process. Once he found out where the explosives were stored, E. J. bypassed the security procedures and took what he wanted. He also knocked out a few students and Ms. Cottaldo, a really cool professor's assistant.

Stealing dangerous material was bad enough. Violence was even worse. Frank and I were gonna bring E. J. down, no matter what it took.

I gunned the Jet Ski's engine and pulled up even with the speedboat. I could just see my brother on the other side of it. With the boat blocking his body, all I could see was Frank's head bobbing up and down with the motion of the ski. Between us, E. J. stood at the controls of the boat, his arm pushing the throttle forward to full speed. From the look on his face, I could tell that the lowlife didn't want to deal with us. He just wanted to get on with his escape up the coast.

But that wasn't going to happen.

We were running our Jet Skis at top speed, making the wind whip around us. The rush of air made any kind of talking impossible. Thankfully, Frank and I had been in more chases than E. J. could even imagine. ATAC always had us saving the day—or at least lots of people—in some way or another. So we had a language all our own.

Frank's arm shot out, pointing to the back of the boat. Meanwhile, he started to pull his Jet Ski farther up alongside the speedboat. He was playing the decoy, getting E. J.'s attention so I could get close without being noticed.

I let my right wrist ease up just a little, cutting the gas enough to let the boat pass me. Then, just before the V-shaped pattern of the wake caught up with me, I gunned it again, pacing the boat and pulling in tight. I didn't want to end up behind the boat—one misstep back there and there'd be one less Hardy in the world to give criminals a hard time.

As my ski pulled up to the starboard side of the boat, I glanced up to make sure E. J.'s attention was still on Frank. Boy, was it. E. J. still had one hand on the throttle, but in his other hand he held a gun!

He pointed it at Frank. Frank serpentined on his Jet Ski, weaving so close to the boat that E. J. couldn't get a clear shot, then pulling back out again to keep his attention. It was a dangerous game of cat and mouse my brother was playing. But Frank could handle it. He may be a little boring at times, but the dude has nerves of steel.

I turned my attention back to what I was doing. I had to get on that boat. It would have to be a precision maneuver. In order to reach the back of the boat, I would have to jump from farther up alongside it. Because the moment I left the Jet Ski and leaped into the air, I would start to slow down. Which meant the boat would move ahead of me. If I didn't time it just right, I'd end up leaping into the water in the boat's wake. Or, worse, I'd end up jumping into the engine itself. Once again, one less Hardy.

I studied the metal railing that ran along the edge of the boat. That's what I was shooting for. But to get there, I had to stand up and take my hands off the controls of my Jet Ski. Even without the wind whizzing by, the sound of the boat's engine roaring, and the bouncing up and down of the waves, it would have been a challenging leap. But with all of that going on, it was going to be nearly impossible.

And I had only one shot.

I leaned left, steering as close to the boat as I could. I paced myself to the boat, with my Jet Ski about five feet in front of where I wanted to land. I took a deep breath and wished my Jet Ski well, since I was going to have to ditch it here in the open water.

Time to rock and roll.

I stood up on the Jet Ski, keeping both hands on the handlebars to steady myself. I glanced at the railing to get a feel for the distance. In one motion, I released the Jet Ski and leaped toward the railing. The Jet Ski engine stopped its racing and fell back. I saw the boat speeding by as I flew through the air. It was almost past me!

At the very last second I grabbed the railing, my hands wrapping around the cool metal. My wrists, elbows, and shoulders jerked hard as the force of the boat pulled me along. I was dragging all my weight with just my arms—but I had reached the boat.

Made it!

Now for the *really* hard part. My feet dangled just inches above the racing water, and the wind whipping past threatened to yank me free of the railing. My biceps ached as I struggled to pull myself up onto the boat. Man, did I appreciate all those chin-ups in gym class now. I got my feet up to the level of the deck and threw my left leg over the side. Using all my strength, I pulled myself into the stern of the boat. I landed on my side and sucked in a huge breath of air.

I like to think of myself as pretty nimble and light on my feet. But I guess I make a pretty loud thud when I land. Who knew? I looked up to find E. J. no longer distracted by my brother. Staring over his shoulder at me, he was obviously very aware that I'd boarded his boat. And with my Jet Ski quickly vanishing in the distance, I had no way off. E. J. trained his gun on me.

I leaped to my feet and scanned the boat. There weren't a lot of options. Speedboats don't come with many places to hide. "Back to where I came from," I whispered to myself. It wasn't a good option, but it was the only one I had. I would get back onto the running board next to the engine at the stern of the boat. That would at least put the railing between the two of us and give me something to hold on to. I could duck down there and maybe—just maybe—not get shot.

I took one last look at E. J. All I saw was the muzzle of the gun pointing straight at me. I was out of time. I threw myself over the back railing in a tight dive roll.

I landed on the wooden planking of the running board, face-to-face with the engine. Or at least face-to-motor. My fingers grabbed the small space between the boards, stopping me inches from the roiling water and, underneath, the rotor. My eyes focused on the fuel line that fed gas into the engine.

Excellent! We could leave this bird dead in the water. I reached into my back pocket for my trusted Swiss Army knife. I'd have to clean the salt water and fuel off the blade later, but it would be worth it. Just as I flicked open the blade, though, I heard the engine cut out. Why was E. J. stopping?

With the engine down, Frank's voice cut through the sound of his Jet Ski. "Joe—hurry! E. J.'s coming this way!"

Frank was running the ski right next to me, slowing to stay even with the slowing speedboat. I started sawing through the fuel line. It was tougher than I expected. I pressed harder.

"Don't saw at it, Joe," Frank yelled. "Just stab it and pull the knife out."

I grabbed the fuel line and wrapped my hand around it in a fist. I pulled it taut and brought the knife down, point first. If I didn't hit it dead center, the blade would just skim off the side.

But then, I've always had good aim. Perfect. Fuel shot everywhere.

I stood up, ready to launch myself onto Frank's Jet Ski and take off.

"Freeze right there, kid." I turned to look at E. J., who was standing above me on the deck, gun aiming at me from point-blank range. "I don't know what you boys think you're doing. But now you are in a world of trouble," he snarled. "See, I'm not much into kids. And I'm even less into nosy kids. So we've got a problem."

"No," Frank replied coolly. "*You've* got a problem." Frank's Jet Ski bobbed next to the speedboat. He sat back, a lighter burning in his hand. "You're standing on a boat with fuel running all over the place and a hold full of explosives. That about sum it up, Joe?"

Frank looked at me and gave me the slightest nod of his head. I winked at him to show I understood. He wanted me to jump onto his Jet Ski when he gave the word.

"That sounds about right to me, Frank." I used the excuse of answering him to position my feet to get the best jumping leverage possible.

"So before we negotiate any further . . ." Frank gave me another warning look. We were almost there. "Maybe you should put down that gun. Now!"

When he said that word, several things happened at once. My brother swung his arm violently, hurling the lighter at the boat. I took one step onto the top of the engine and leaped onto Frank's Jet Ski. And E. J., in a fit of self-preservation, ran toward the starboard side and dove over the railing of the boat into the water.

Once I landed on the Jet Ski and got my arms around him for safety, Frank took off at top speed, back to the shore. I ducked down, waiting for the explosion.

It never came.

"What happened?" I yelled into my brother's ear as I leaned against him to stay on the speeding Jet Ski.

Frank turned his head and yelled back, "Lighters don't stay lit if you take your thumb off the gas lever! It's only old-style lighters that do." Frank smiled at me. "Can't believe you didn't know that."

I responded the only way a little brother can in that situation. "Shut up!"

By the time we reached shore, a police boat was going after E. J.

Frank and I high-fived. Another successful ATAC mission. There was no feeling like it.

FRANK

2
Kung Fu Fighting

"You two made it back just in time. You were almost too late." Dad rushed out to greet us as we pulled into the driveway of our big house on our bikes. That's my all-time favorite perk of being a secret ATAC operative—Joe and I both have super-cool, state-of-the-art motorcycles. If you've ever dreamed of a high-tech gadget that could go on a bike, our motorcycles have it.

I yanked my helmet off. "What's wrong?" From the tone of Dad's voice, it sounded like an urgent ATAC type of problem.

"Did E. J. have an accomplice? Is someone here?" Joe was already off his bike, looking around for trouble.

11

Dad is the only one of the adults in our family who knows we're with ATAC. And he only knows because he was one of the founders of American Teens Against Crime. After he retired from the New York City police force, he'd come up with the idea of using teenagers to help fight crime on the local level all across the country. But the way he worries about Joe and me, I figure he sometimes thinks he did the wrong thing by recruiting us to the agency.

He grabbed my overly alert brother by the collar and pulled him in for a hug to muffle what he was saying. "Shhh! No. Your mother's about to go off to a conference for the next week. She's been calling you on your cell phones and waiting for you to get back." He whispered over Joe's shoulder so only the two of us could hear.

I grimaced. I'd been so focused on our mission that I'd totally spaced on Mom's trip.

Behind Dad, Mom and Aunt Trudy came out of the house, each lugging a large suitcase.

"Boys, you made it back!" Mom's face broke into a huge smile. She was excited to see us.

Aunt Trudy frowned at us. "Where have you been?" she cried. "Your poor mother has been worried sick thinking she might not see you before she left." No one could try to make you feel guilty with as much self-confidence as Aunt Trudy. If only we could tell her we were protecting our nation's coastline!

"That's not important. We need to get your mother on the road, so go wish her a good conference," Dad intervened. He's smooth when it comes to keeping our cover.

Joe smiled broadly and hurried across the front lawn to Mom. "Sorry we're so late. We got caught up . . ."

He'd gotten ahead of himself—as usual—and didn't have a full excuse in mind. That's my brother. His philosophy is always leap first, and look later.

". . . at school," he finished lamely.

Mom is a research librarian with a giant, always accessible hard drive for a brain. My brother and I know we're always tempting fate trying to pull the wool over her eyes. Good thing Dad's there to step in with a cover when we need it. Without his help, she would have found out about ATAC ages ago!

"Since you're finally back, you boys can carry these bags," Aunt Trudy huffed at us, still put out. "I'm going to go in and see about making you something to eat." She turned and tromped purposefully into the house. Joe and I laughed. So did

Mom. Once Aunt Trudy started pushing food on us, we all knew she'd forgiven whatever horrible thing we'd done to get on her bad side.

"Here, Mom, let me get that." Joe reached out and took the bag Mom was dragging. He nearly fell over from the weight. "Whoa!"

I reached down to pick up the bag that Aunt Trudy had abandoned. It was really heavy too. "How long is this conference you're going to, Mom?" I swung the suitcase up and followed Joe to the Volvo. It sagged noticeably when we put the suitcases into the trunk.

"Just a week." Mom came over to make sure the bags were safe inside. "But there are all kinds of source materials I'll need to read to keep up with the lectures."

"And by 'source materials,' you mean bowling balls and cast iron pans, right?" Joe asked as she fussed with the suitcases, tugging on the zippers to make sure they were shut.

"Your mother is being modest," Dad said. "She's not just keeping up with the other lectures. She's also presenting one of her own."

"That's great, Mom," I said. "Are you talking to them about the work you've done in cluster analysis improving archival search times?"

Joe stared at me like I was speaking Elvish or something.

"What?" I asked. "With all the information floating around in databases and on the Internet, it's hard to find what you want when you want it. Mom is making serious headway in solving the problem."

Joe rolled his eyes, but Mom beamed at me. "And people say teens never listen to their parents," she said. She gave Dad a hug and a kiss good-bye, then turned to us. "Now, since I know *both* of you are listening: I expect a phone call every night. Be good. And listen to your dad and Aunt Trudy."

"Yeah, Mom," Joe said. "And our bedtime is seven thirty, and we shouldn't eat junk food," he joked.

"Don't worry, honey. Trudy and I will keep them in line." Dad helpfully cut short the "be responsible" portion of the good-bye talk. "Why don't you boys go inside? I think there's a package waiting for you in the living room. Your mother and I have a few more things to talk about before she goes."

"Bye, Mom." I kissed her on the cheek. So did Joe. Dad took Mom's hand and walked her to the car.

We were already speeding toward the house.

"All right! Mystery package for the Hardys," Joe exclaimed happily.

"Yeah—inside with Aunt Trudy," I whispered to him.

Joe's eyes widened. "I guess we better go ATAC it!" He elbowed me in the ribs, faking a laugh, and ran into the house.

I rolled my eyes and followed my superlame comedian brother inside.

On the kitchen table sat a large box wrapped in brown paper.

"Stupid bird! Off the box! Stupid bird! Off the box!" Our parrot Playback shuffled back and forth along the edge of the package, keeping his eyes fixed on Aunt Trudy. She took a step toward the box. Playback flung out his wings, puffing the feathers out and squawking loudly. She stepped back with a cry. Joe and I chuckled. Trudy and Playback have a love/hate relationship. This didn't seem to be a "love" day.

"Who's sending you boys such big packages?" Aunt Trudy demanded. The sandwiches she'd come in to make for us lay half prepared on the counter. Curiosity had obviously gotten the better of her. Thankfully Playback had been there to keep her at bay.

"Well . . . um . . . I think probably it's . . ." Nothing sprang to mind. I knew this package had come from ATAC. Which meant I had no idea at all what was in the box. It could be anything. And, more importantly, whatever it was shouldn't opened in front of Aunt Trudy.

This time Joe had more luck than me in coming up with a white lie for Aunt Trudy. "It's just something we sent away for. We'll open it upstairs. I'm sure you don't want it cluttering up the kitchen." He stepped up to the box and shooed Playback off of it. Playback flapped to the back of one of the kitchen chairs and began to chant, "Open it. Open it."

"Why not just open it here?" With Playback safely off the box, Aunt Trudy was bolder. "Anything two teen boys send away for should probably be opened in front of one responsible adult. Here, let me get the tape." She pulled the kitchen shears out of a nearby drawer.

Joe and I stood helpless as she cut through the brown tape sealing the box. We looked at each other, panicked. This was worse than nearly getting shot by E. J.

"There you go." Aunt Trudy stepped back, leaving us to unpack our own disaster. "Did you get what you wanted?"

We had no choice. Slowly I reached out and

opened the top flaps of the box. *Please let it be something innocent looking,* I thought.

I glanced down and saw two white karate outfits with white belts.

I don't know what I was expecting, but not this. As I lifted the uniforms from the box, Joe reached in and pulled out a karate book and a martial-arts-themed video game. Other karate gear had been packed in under the book—exercise mats for falling and sparring gloves.

"Yeah, Aunt Trudy, this is pretty much what we ordered. It's, um . . . karate stuff," I finished, hoping there would be no further inquiry.

"I can see that. But why?" Aunt Trudy never backed down easily.

"Actually, Trudy, this is my doing," Dad said, coming into the kitchen just in time. "The boys mentioned they were interested in learning more about martial arts, so I ordered them this stuff online."

"I thought you boys said you sent away for this karate . . . paraphernalia," Aunt Trudy said to Joe. I had to hand it to her—you couldn't slip anything past Trudy.

But Dad recovered quickly. "They were covering for me. I told them you might not be happy with them learning to fight."

"Yeah," I said teasingly. "We didn't want Dad to have to face the wrath of Aunt Trudy."

"But the martial arts are all about discipline," Dad went on. "And you always say the boys need more of that, right?"

Aunt Trudy crossed her arms and glared at all three of us. I could tell she felt outnumbered without Mom in the house. "Fine. Learn to fight. Just don't do it in the house." Shaking her head, she turned back to the sandwiches.

Joe gave me a look. He gestured toward the box. For the first time I noticed that there was something else inside. Folded into the pages of the book was a stack of fifty-dollar bills. Joe quickly threw everything back in the box.

"Thanks, Dad." I gave Joe a hand with the box.

Dad shot us a thumbs-up as we quickly left the room.

"We'll be back for sandwiches in a little while, Aunt Trudy," Joe called out as we ran up the stairs to my room.

"I think she's getting more suspicious as she gets older," I said to Joe as I closed my bedroom door behind us. Joe dumped the box down on my bed and immediately pawed through it to find the video game. That's how our ATAC missions come— disguised as games. Joe flipped the disc to me.

"I can't wait to hear what the new mission is," Joe said. "Anything that involves martial arts has got to be cool." He reached in and pulled out the karate robes while I stuck the disc, labeled MARTIAL LAW, into my gaming system. Joe slipped on one of the black jackets and tied the white belt around his waist. "What do you think? Stylin', right?"

I ignored him and watched the monitor. Rows of guys in black uniforms appeared on the screen. In unison, they stepped forward and shot out their right fists. With one voice they cried, "Hy-yah!" An unseen male caller yelled out a command. The boys moved again, pivoting on their front foot and stepping backward with the other. They bent their back legs, moving into a low crouch.

"Martial arts have been practiced as a form of self-discipline and self-defense for centuries," the deep voice of one of the mysterious ATAC mission narrators droned over this scene. Onscreen, the guys shot out of their crouch into a vicious kick. "Hy-yah!" That cry was closer by. I whipped around to find Joe, with sparring gloves on, mimicking the moves from the video.

"Joe, get serious and pay attention." I grabbed his white belt and pulled him to sit down in front of the screen.

"I was watching," he protested.

Onscreen, the camera panned up from the boys to the grand master calling out the moves, and the voice continued: *"There are many types of martial arts—tae kwon do, karate, ninpo taijutsu, kung fu. When taught and learned correctly, they can train the mind as well as the body. When taught and learned with the wrong intent"*—the boys gave an extra loud "HY-YAH!" and the scene faded out to black—*"they can cause great harm."* The screen filtered into an image of a man lying crumpled on the ground.

"The Rising Phoenix Martial Arts School in Holtsville opened its doors just over one year ago." The image of a one-story, stand-alone building appeared. The floor-to-ceiling storefront-style windows allowed a clear view of the dojo inside, where a class of teens worked on one-on-one drills. The entrance doorway had been outfitted with a giant red archway, with golden dragons sitting on either side.

"Shouldn't those be phoenixes?" Joe asked. "I mean, it's not called the Rising *Dragon*."

"*Phoenix* is the plural of phoenix, Joe. And shhh," I replied.

A photograph of an Asian man in his late twenties appeared. *"Paul Huang is the owner and sole proprietor of the Rising Phoenix."* Paul wore a white robe with a black belt and stood in a classic "don't mess with me" Bruce Lee pose. *"Huang teaches karate to the teens of Holtsville and the surrounding towns. Since the Rising Phoenix opened, its student body has grown quickly and now includes over one hundred part-time students of varying skill levels."*

Joe sighed and rolled his eyes. "I feel a giant 'so what' coming on."

"Huang is ambitious. He plans to open a chain of karate studios throughout the Northeast. These plans recently got a significant boost when InSight Investments, a financing group, entered into talks with Huang. It is expected that they will agree to fund his expansion."

Joe faked a sneeze, masking his "So what?"

The announcer answered. *"Over the past month, two students at the Rising Phoenix school have ended up in the hospital."* The screen was filled with pictures of two boys. The one on the left was thin with acne and a mop of dark brown hair, the one on the right was a small boy with neatly cropped blond hair. *"The picture on your left is of John Mangione. A student at Rising Phoenix since it opened, John collapsed last week and was clinically dead for a few moments before his heart was restarted. Russell Olwell turned up at the local emergency room badly beaten a few days ago."*

I shot a look at Joe. He'd dropped his attitude

and was paying close attention. "If kids are getting hurt because of this school, a whole chain of them could be a disaster," I said.

"Your mission is to look into the school. We here at ATAC believe it is more than simple coincidence that two students of this school were badly hurt. You boys have to get close to the school and find out if it is dangerous before Paul Huang succeeds in expanding it."

"Now *these* are the kind of lessons I can get into." Joe jumped back up and into his pseudo-karate moves. I had to agree with him. Math lessons were okay and all, but karate lessons? *Much* cooler.

"This mission, like every mission, is top secret," the announcer finished. *"In five seconds, this disc will be reformatted into a regular CD."*

Five seconds later, Carl Douglas's 1970s hit "Kung Fu Fighting" blared from the computer's speakers.

3

Dis-Orientation

"Cool bikes," a scrawny, nerdy-looking boy called out the second we pulled up to the Rising Phoenix Martial Arts School on our motorcycles. The kid wore a backpack full of textbooks that threatened to pull him over backward. He looked to be a couple of years younger than us and was probably sixty pounds lighter.

"Thanks," Frank replied. "I'm Frank. This is my brother, Joe." I gave him a little wave, since I was in the middle of locking my bike up.

"I'm Billy Lee. That's Billy, and then Lee. Lee's my last name. So it's not Bill-Lee-Lee-Lee. . . ." Billy needed to take a breath to continue, giving me the opportunity to cut in.

"Got it. Billy. Say, who do we see about signing up for classes here?" I asked quickly.

"Oh, that would be Finn. Mr. Campbell. He lets us call him Finn. He runs the place for Sensei Huang." Billy walked toward the glass doors of the building, pointing. Between the golden dragons, we could see a tall desk with a man behind it.

"Are you going inside?" Frank asked Billy.

"Sure. Yes. I'm a student here," Billy said proudly.

"Cool—then you're the guy who can give us the inside scoop," Frank said, trying to make friends. "We'll find you inside in a few!"

"Okay." Billy started walking backward, squinting at us and our bikes like we were criminals ourselves. "I'll see you in the locker room, okay?" Only when he tripped over the curb at the edge of the parking lot and nearly fell did he turn and walk inside.

"I think we can safely exclude Bill Lee-Lee-Lee there from our list of suspects," I pointed out with a smile. "Nice kid, but he doesn't seem the criminal mastermind type."

Frank smiled too. "No, but he does jump right up on the list of most likely to need protection, don't you think?"

I nodded.

"Do you have the cash for the classes?" Frank asked quietly.

I patted my wallet. "Right here. I'm kind of hoping they have an introductory sale so we can use the extra cash for pizza later."

"Yeah, that'd be nice, but fat chance. ATAC always knows precisely how much a mission will cost." Frank nodded toward the door. "When we go in, you scope the place and I'll do the talking."

"Got it." I handed the cash over to Frank so he could pay.

We walked between the golden dragons and under the giant red archway. That's when I saw it. "First mystery solved," I said. Behind the dragons, behind the archway, out of sight from the ATAC camera in the case brief we were sent, a giant golden phoenix soared over the double doorway, standing guard. At least I assumed it was a phoenix, since I've never actually seen one.

"Happy now?" Frank asked, holding the door for me to enter.

"Definitely."

Everything was quiet and peaceful inside the Rising Phoenix. Frank and I stepped into the tiled entryway, greeted by slightly dimmed lights and soft sitar music piped in from somewhere. Water rained down over a bamboo-encircled Buddha in a fountain to our left.

But as muted and subdued as it was, this was

still clearly a place of business. Along the right side of the entryway ran a glass case with "Rising Phoenix"–branded headbands, robes, sparring gloves, and so on. Finn Campbell, the man Billy Lee had pointed out, stood directly in front of us.

Frank strode confidently up to Finn while I trailed a bit behind. I pretended to be looking at the "Rising Phoenix" daggers and throwing stars in the case, although I was really looking over the case through thick glass into what must be the school's office. I noticed windows leading to the outside— to the back of the building. Those could come in handy later. You never know when you might need a quick escape.

"Hi. We'd like to take some classes." Frank pulled Finn away from some paperwork he was doing. He looked Frank over suspiciously, which gave me the chance to do the same to him. He was a pretty normal-looking guy in his thirties. Balding and pasty-faced, he looked more like an intellectual than a fighter.

Apparently deciding we were okay, he switched into sales mode. "Great. You've come to the right place. Sensei Huang is a great teacher, and as you can see, we have all-new facilities." Finn gestured to our left. Through an archway, we could see the dojo, a large room with a fully padded floor. In one corner, several kids worked on a hanging punching bag. In another, two pairs of guys moved through choreographed maneuvers. In the middle, a girl stretched alone.

"We have a special introductory deal right now. . . ." He stopped and laughed in a self-deprecating manner, which I totally didn't buy. "But I'm getting ahead of myself. I'm Finn Campbell. Please, call me Finn." He smiled broadly, all teeth, and extended his hand.

"I'm Frank Hardy. And this is my brother, Joe." Frank shook his hand.

I stepped up and grabbed his hand too. "Hi." A single pump shake, and out. It was the shake of a man who prided himself on efficiency.

"Glad to meet you both. As I was saying . . ." Finn slid a glossy pamphlet across the counter for Frank and me to look at. I peeked into the dojo and took a step inside. "Joe—make sure you don't walk on the mat with your shoes, okay? Just stick to the tiled area for now. And I'll need you back here for some paperwork in a minute," Finn called after me. Without missing a beat, he turned back to Frank. "We have a ten-lesson introductory offer, with the first class being free. How does that sound?"

"Perfect. We'll need ten lessons each." Frank sounded genuinely enthusiastic.

"Now," Finn continued in full swing, "let's see if you need any of our genuine Rising Phoenix equipment. . . ."

That was all I could take of the sales pitch. I stepped into the dojo, careful to avoid the mat. The tile ran along the sides to the back of the dojo, straight to two heavy wooden doors. I assumed these were the locker rooms. Walking toward them, I was surprised to find a hallway to my right. The hallway ran behind the entryway and Finn Campbell's desk and seemed to lead to the office that I'd seen. I took a turn and headed toward the door.

Inside the office, Paul Huang was talking with a student. I recognized him immediately from the ATAC video. I could only just see him over the student. He wasn't a large man, but he didn't look like someone I wanted to tangle with.

Something about the student Paul Huang was talking to was very familiar. I could only see him from the back, so I couldn't tell who it was.

Before I could place him, though, Frank came up behind me. "Okay, we're in. But we need to go change. Orientation starts in a few minutes," he said, pulling me by the shoulder toward the locker rooms.

The boys' locker room was pretty basic—wooden benches, metal lockers, a vague smell of sweat. There were a few other kids there getting changed. Some of them looked as if they couldn't figure out exactly how to put on the karate uniform. All of them looked kind of . . . awkward. Maybe even dorky. It was weird.

"It's called a *gi*," I heard Billy Lee say. I followed his voice around a row of lockers to find him lecturing an overweight kid who was halfway dressed in a Rising Phoenix karate uniform.

"A gee?" the overweight kid repeated doubtfully.

"Yes. Traditionally there was no real uniform for karate, but when the discipline entered the modern age, the *gi* was adopted as the uniform of choice," Billy said.

I bit back a smile. It was obvious: Billy Lee was a karate geek.

"So Billy, you know a lot about this stuff," I said. I grabbed an open locker nearby and tossed my jacket and shoes inside. "How long have you been taking classes here?"

"Two months," Billy said. "But I found out all the history stuff myself. I like to know the background of any new hobby I start." His cheeks turned red.

"That's cool," I assured him.

"I think so. Anyway, Sensei Huang doesn't talk about that—he's more into putting karate to use in our everyday lives."

That sounded a little weird. "You mean fighting people for real?" I asked.

"No. Well, not unless you need to," Billy said.

"Why would you need to?" I asked. Billy looked way too small to have any chance in a fight, no matter how much karate he knew.

"Just, you know . . ." Billy took a step closer and lowered his voice. "Like there's this jerk at my school. He's been pushing me around since I was little. And when I told Sensei Huang about it, he offered to give me private lessons."

I shot Frank a look, and he raised his eyebrows. "Private lessons, so you could fight this bully?" Frank asked.

Billy frowned. "Not really. He said private lessons would make me more adept and quick. You know, so I could have the self-confidence to stand up for myself."

"That sounds good," the overweight kid added. "I'm sick of people making fun of me." He finished tying his white belt and headed off toward the dojo.

I pulled out my *gi* and began to put it on. So did Frank.

"So you must know all about Sensei Huang's background, huh?" Frank casually asked Billy. "Since you do so much research."

"Nah. I couldn't find any info on him," Billy said. "But I don't care. He's a great teacher. And he's really into Eastern medicine and stuff. He's giving me some Chinese herbs to help me bulk up and to keep me focused."

I couldn't help but notice that Billy was still dressed in his khakis and button-down shirt. "Aren't you gonna change?" I asked.

"Oh. No, today's just for orientation," Billy said. "The beginners' class doesn't meet until Tuesday. But it's cool that you guys are joining!"

"What are you doing here, then?" Frank asked.

"Sensei Huang asked me to come in today and talk to Finn." Billy shrugged. "Maybe my mom is late with the tuition check or something."

"Ready, Frank?" I asked.

He nodded. "Let's go."

"Have a good class, you guys," Billy said with a shy smile. "I'll see you on Tuesday."

"Later, Billy," I said. "It was good to meet you."

Frank and I went out into the dojo. The overweight boy from the locker room sat on the mats with five other kids. They all nodded and smiled at us when we came in, except for the one girl. She sat by herself at the back of the room and didn't even bother to look at us. One of the boys and the girl looked around my age, but the rest of them were younger. I was surprised to see that none of them looked very athletic. They were all either too skinny or too heavy, and most of them seemed kind of small. I glanced over at my brother. He was at least six inches taller than every other kid in the room.

I hope we don't stand out too much in the beginners' class, I thought. The mission would be doomed if we couldn't manage to stay undercover. We sat down on the mats and tried to look smaller.

As soon as our butts hit the floor, the office door opened and Paul Huang came out. I wondered if he'd been watching the dojo through his window.

"Welcome," Huang said in a quiet voice. "I'm Paul Huang, the sensei of this school. I'm glad to see you all here at the Rising Phoenix." As he talked, he looked every one of us in the eye, holding each student's gaze for a few seconds before moving on.

That was an old cop's technique, I knew. Dad always said that making eye contact was the easiest way to assert yourself and show your strength. Huang had it down.

"I'm sure all of you have an idea of what it means to study karate," Huang was saying. "Some people think karate is about fighting. But it's not. It's about discipline." He stared at the overweight boy. "Self-discipline."

A thin, gangly boy raised his hand. "We're not gonna learn to kick and fight?" he asked in a nasal voice.

"You will," Huang said. "But those are only moves. The more important lesson you will learn is to trust yourself. To control your body with your mind. The true martial artist will rarely fight, because he—or she—will rarely need to. The true martial artist projects an aura of strength that makes him intimidating to others."

I wasn't quite sure he was right about that, but then again, my martial arts training was limited to playing video games and watching Jackie Chan movies.

"How do you get that aura?" the girl asked. I was surprised to hear her speak up—she was sitting with her knees pulled up to her chest, and she still hadn't looked at anyone else. I'd assumed she was supershy.

Sensei Huang smiled. "Like I said, discipline. Self-control leads to self-confidence. Self-confidence leads to self-esteem. And that leads to greater happiness in all areas of your life. Trust me, everyone. Once you know how to control your body, you'll know how to control your whole life."

I had to force myself not to roll my eyes. I'd expected a karate master to be breaking wooden boards with his bare hands, not giving us a touchy-feely speech about self-confidence. But looking around the room, I noticed the other kids nodding, their eyes shining. Obviously they didn't share my annoyance at Sensei Huang's lecture. And it wasn't too hard to figure out why. These kids all seemed perfectly nice. But they weren't exactly the type of people who ended up popular in school. They could all probably use a self-esteem boost.

So maybe Sensei Huang's method wasn't so bad after all.

"Let me explain how a typical class will go here at the Rising Phoenix," Huang went on. He waved us all to our feet. "We begin with the traditional Japanese bow, to show our respect for each other and for the art of karate." He gave a little bow.

I bowed back. The other kids glanced at me and did the same.

Sensei Huang met my eyes and smiled a little, but I got the sense that he was studying me. I quickly looked down. I didn't want to draw too much attention to myself. From the corner of my eye, I could see Frank staring at his feet too.

"In the beginners' class, we will be studying *kihon*," Huang said. "These are the basic building blocks of karate: striking, blocking, kicking, and punching."

He went on describing the types of moves we would have to learn before we could continue on to more advanced karate. As he talked, I glanced around at the other students. They were all listening intently. I let my gaze wander over to the huge windows at the side of the room. Billy Lee stood out in the hallway, talking to Finn. That was no big surprise—but the look on Billy's face was.

The kid was practically crying. His face was bright red, and he kept shaking his head while Finn talked to him.

I couldn't drag my eyes away from Billy. He'd been so happy in the locker room and outside. What could have happened to make him so upset now?

Billy tried to say something, but Finn cut him off. Finally Billy just turned and ran for the front door. I thought I saw him brush away a tear as he went.

Finn Campbell turned and looked right into the dojo, his eyes on Sensei Huang.

I glanced at the sensei. Huang was staring back at Finn with an alert expression on his face. I got the feeling that he'd been watching the whole exchange. But he just kept giving his introduction speech without missing a beat.

This guy is smooth, I thought.

"Enough talk," Huang said suddenly. "I'm sure you'd all like a demonstration of a few of these moves we're discussing."

The other kids all nodded, so I did too.

"Okay, I'm going to show you a basic combination. You'll have to master all these moves before you can advance out of the beginners' class," Huang explained. "I need some help to demonstrate this, so I've asked one of my top students to join us."

He waved to the back of the room. I turned, surprised. I hadn't noticed anybody come into the dojo.

And when I saw the top student who was coming up to help Huang, my surprise turned to outright shock. Because there, in all his gawky, shy glory, was one of my best friends: Chet Morton!

4
Nerd Master

I couldn't believe it! Chet, at the Rising Phoenix? It made no sense. Chet's a great guy and all, but he's not exactly brave. Or strong. Or athletic. And right now, he stood in front of the class blinking furiously with one eye and making weird faces.

When Sensei Huang raised his hand and did a lunge punch—his fist flying straight at Chet's face—I almost ran up there to stop him. I mean, it was Chet! What could he do to defend himself?

But when Huang's fist got close to his head, Chet brought his arm up in a blocking move that kept Huang from hitting him. Next, Huang spun and kicked Chet in the chest. This time Chet went down. Still, even as he hit the ground, I could see he wasn't hurt. In fact, it seemed like Huang's foot had barely touched him. Just like that first punch had seemed designed to hit the air in front of Chet's nose, rather than actually hitting Chet.

I breathed a sigh of relief. Huang was doing all the real work. All Chet had to do was show off one basic block, then fall down. And I knew from years of experience with Chet that he was good at falling down.

Everyone in the dojo gasped. Chet climbed back to his feet and bowed at Huang. The other kids all clapped as if that had been some serious karate. Obviously they hadn't been watching as closely as I had.

I shot a glance at Joe. He nodded. He'd seen what I'd seen.

"Thanks, Chet," Huang said.

Chet grinned from ear to ear and practically bounced back into the group of students. He was still blinking, but he headed toward the back of the dojo, looking proud of himself. I noticed the one girl in class smiling at him, her eyes shining. She stepped up really close to Chet as he walked by her. Now, I'm not too comfortable around girls. My brain just shuts off and I tend to act like a total dork. But compared to Chet? I'm Brad Pitt.

Chet doesn't just act dorky around girls. He acts

oblivious. As if he's not even aware that there *are* girls on the planet. I don't think I've ever seen him talk to a girl in our whole lives—and today was no exception. Chet noticed the girl smiling at him and he took off, fleeing back into the hallway that led to Huang's office.

"That's it for our orientation," Huang was saying. "If anyone has questions, I'll be happy to answer them one on one. Otherwise, I'll see you all on Tuesday."

I caught Joe watching me and shrugged. We both knew we should be talking to Huang. He's the one we were here to investigate, after all. But we also both knew that we just had to talk to Chet ASAP. We had to know what he was doing in a martial arts school!

Joe and I left Huang fielding questions from two of the other kids. We took off after Chet and caught up to him in the locker room changing out of his *gi*.

"Hey, Chet," I said, patting him on the back. "What's going on?"

He jumped, then grinned when he saw us. "What are you guys doing here?" he asked, shoving his glasses up higher on his nose.

"Didn't you see us in the beginners' lecture?" Joe asked.

"No," Chet said. "Were you there? I couldn't see much. I can't wear my glasses during karate. Too dangerous, you know? They might get cracked."

"How can you do karate if you can't see well?" I asked.

"Oh, I usually put in contact lenses. But I washed one down the sink before. So I had to do the whole demo with only one lens in."

That explains the bizarro blinking, I thought. Poor Chet had really bad luck.

"I can never get the stupid things in right," Chet muttered out loud. "I don't understand why everybody loves them so much. What's wrong with glasses?"

Joe clapped him on the back. "You did a pretty impressive job up there, considering you couldn't see."

"Yeah. What are you, a brown belt already?" I joked.

Chet blushed. "I hardly had to do anything," he admitted. "Sensei Huang does all the work."

"He must like you," Joe said. "He said you're one of his top students."

Chet puffed up like a peacock. "I *am* a fast learner," he said. "You guys will be joining my class, I guess. I'm kinda surprised you're here."

"How come?" I asked.

"Just, you know, the two of you always act so sure of yourselves. I wouldn't expect you to take a class like this."

"Well, I thought we were just learning karate. I didn't expect all the self-esteem stuff," Joe complained.

"Yeah. Sensei Huang has a pretty unique approach," Chet said. "Do you want to meet him?"

"Definitely," I said.

Chet led us out of the locker room and back into the hallway. The girl from class was hanging around near one of the office doors. Her whole face lit up when she saw Chet.

"Hi, Chet!" she chirped.

"Oh. Um, hi," Chet mumbled. He seemed shocked that she was talking to him.

"You know, we didn't really meet in class," Joe said, smiling at her. "Why don't you introduce us, Chet?"

I nudged him with my elbow. Poor Chet was obviously uncomfortable with this girl. Why did Joe have to torture him like this?

"Um . . . uh . . . Frank and Joe Hardy, this is Liz Campbell," Chet stammered.

Immediately my brain clicked back into ATAC mode, and I could see that Joe's did too. "Campbell?" I asked. "Are you related to Finn?"

Liz nodded. "He's my dad."

SUSPECT PROFILE

Name: Paul Huang

Hometown: Philadelphia, PA

Physical description: Age 26, 5'9", 170 lbs. of lean, mean, fighting machine. Short dark hair, brown eyes. Asian American. Never wears any expression other than calm and controlled. Has a tattoo of a Chinese dragon on his forearm.

Occupation: Owns the Rising Phoenix Martial Arts School in Holtsville. Is the only sensei. Plans to expand the Rising Phoenix brand into a nationwide chain of karate training centers.

Background: Grew up in Philadelphia with a reputation for brawling and pickpocketing. Found his calling when he took his first karate class at age 16.

Suspicious behavior: Two students at his school have ended up in the hospital in the past month.

Suspected of: Causing harm to students? He's the only link between the two injured boys.

Possible motive: Wants to be in control, no matter what it takes.

"That's cool," Joe said. "He must be psyched that you're into karate, huh? I mean, he obviously is, or else he wouldn't work here."

Liz's smile vanished. Suddenly she looked more like the sullen girl we'd first seen in the dojo. "Not really," she said. "I mean, he isn't that excited about me taking lessons. He's afraid something will happen to me."

I shot a look at Joe. Why was Finn afraid? Did he know something about the students who'd gotten hurt?

"I don't care, though. He can't tell me what to do. Sensei Huang said I could take lessons." Liz stuck her chin in the air defiantly and walked off to the girls' locker room.

Chet was sweating bullets. He looked relieved that she was gone. Of course, Joe took that as a cue to tease him.

"So that's your girlfriend, hmmm?" he asked, wiggling his eyebrows.

"No!" Chet yelped.

I pushed Joe in the shoulder, and he responded by dropping into a boxing stance and doing a few fake jabs at me.

"Looks like you two already know how to fight," Paul Huang's voice broke in.

I spun around, startled. I hadn't heard him come up. He was gazing at Joe and me with a strange look on his face.

"Sensei, these are two of my best friends," Chet said eagerly. "Frank and Joe Hardy."

I held out my hand, and he shook it. His grasp was firm, and I noticed a small tattoo on his forearm—a Chinese dragon. When I looked into his eyes, I got the feeling that he was trying to read me, see what I was all about.

He did the same to Joe.

"You boys go to school with Chet?" Huang asked.

"Yep. Ever since second grade," Joe said.

"And are you in the same clubs and activities?" Huang pressed. "What did you tell me, Chet? Science Club and the debate team?"

"Frank and I are more into sports," Joe said. I wanted to kick him—obviously Huang didn't want jocks here. We were the only students in the whole place who didn't seem athletically challenged.

"Hmm. In that case, you're not the kind of students I usually attract," Huang said, confirming my suspicions. "I'm more interested in finding teenagers who feel that they're not good at sports—kids who think of themselves as clumsy or uncoordinated. Those are the ones I like to help. Whenever I can teach someone a skill to be proud of, I'm happy."

Joe looked panicked, so I stepped in. "Sports are really more Joe's thing," I said quickly. "I've always been a little embarrassed when I try to play. I . . . uh . . . drop the ball a lot in baseball. That kind of thing."

"And he's a terrible hitter," Joe agreed.

I'd get him for that later!

"I guess what I mean is that I don't think I'm a bad athlete. I just get self-conscious when I know people are watching me. And that makes me klutzy."

This was hard, pretending to be insecure. One thing our parents always drilled into Joe and me was that we could do anything we set our minds to. I was starting to realize how unusual that kind of self-confidence was. Suddenly I felt lucky. But I also felt like we might have blown our chance to go undercover here at the Rising Phoenix.

Did Huang buy my story?

He studied me for a long time, then smiled. "I think you'll find that karate gives you a certain inner balance, Frank," he said. "It will keep your focus on what you're doing, not on who's watching you."

I smiled gratefully. I kinda thought that was a good opportunity for us to get out of there and let Huang forget about us for a while, but Joe pushed on.

"Sensei, what is your training?" he asked. "Did you go to school here?"

Huang looked at his watch. "I have extensive training, Joe, but unfortunately I don't have time to talk about it right now. Maybe another time." He gave us a farewell nod and disappeared into his office.

"Isn't he cool?" Chet said as we headed back into the locker room to grab our stuff.

"Yeah. He doesn't talk about himself much, though," Joe commented.

On the way outside, Chet pulled me aside. "I never knew you felt self-conscious playing sports, Frank," he said.

I felt bad for lying to my friend, but what could I do? We were here on a mission, and that meant lying sometimes. "Not as self-conscious as I feel around girls," I joked.

"I hear you." Chet gave us a wave and walked

over to his mother's car. She was parked near the curb, waiting for him.

Joe and I hopped on our motorcycles and pulled on our helmets. "What do you think?" my brother asked before we took off.

"I think Huang is a little too weird for me," I said. "I don't know what he's up to, but I get the feeling it's something we won't like."

5
Too Quiet

"And where do you boys think you're going at this hour?" Aunt Trudy demanded on Monday morning.

Busted!

I turned around, tucking my motorcycle helmet under my arm. The kitchen clock said 6:35. Who knew our aunt got up so early?

"To school," Frank said, looking innocent the way only he can.

Aunt Trudy snorted. "School doesn't start for an hour and a half," she pointed out.

"Early birds! Early birds!" Playback chimed in.

"Yeah, but we have a project due at the end of the week," I said. "We want to get some time in on it before classes this morning."

Aunt Trudy frowned. "Since when do you two have a class together?"

Frank shot me a look, and I shrugged. So I didn't always think through my cover stories. So what? Frank always came up with a way to save me.

"It's not a class project, Aunt Trudy," he said. "It's for the Science Club. We're working on an experiment with Chet, and we need to get into the lab so we can use the equipment before the chem classes need it."

Aunt Trudy kept right on frowning. She does that a lot. "Did you eat breakfast?" she demanded.

"No," I admitted. Frank shook his head.

"Well, at least take a banana." Aunt Trudy shoved one at Frank and one at me. "And get yourselves some orange juice when you get to school."

"We will. Thanks!" I was out the door before she could think of any more questions to ask us.

In a minute we were on our bikes and heading for the South Coast Hospital. Visiting hours started at seven and we wanted to be there. We had to talk to John Mangione. He was the first Rising Phoenix student who'd ended up hurt.

Unfortunately, the nurse didn't want to let us upstairs. "Are you family?" he asked, looking us up and down.

"Well, no," I replied. "We're friends of John's."

"No visitors except family," the nurse said, and he went back to reading his morning paper.

Great.

I glanced around. The nurse's station was right in front of the elevators. There was no way we could sneak by this guy.

"But we're here on behalf of everyone at John's martial arts school," I told him. "All the kids chipped in and bought him a present, and we're supposed to deliver it." I held up my backpack as if there was a gift inside. I just hoped the nurse didn't ask to see it.

He squinted at the backpack, then looked back at me. I did my best to look as sweet and innocent as my brother.

And it worked!

"Oh, all right," the nurse grumbled. He checked a chart in front of him. "Room 1603. Don't stay too long."

"We won't, sir. Thank you," Frank said. I hit the up button on the elevator. Soon enough we were face-to-face with John Mangione. He looked pretty wasted. His skin was pale and waxy, and his eyes were bloodshot. Still, he wasn't as small and thin as the photo on the ATAC disc had made him look. In fact, he was pretty buff. Before he'd ended up in the hospital, he was probably a strong guy.

"Do I know you?" John asked. He crossed his arms and looked at us suspiciously.

"No. I'm Joe Hardy and this is my brother, Frank," I said. "We're students at the Rising Phoenix."

John squinted. I could tell he was trying to place us.

"We're also sort of amateur detectives," Frank said. That's our typical cover story—we never tell anyone about ATAC. It's top secret. "And we have a feeling there's something strange going down at the Rising Phoenix."

"I wouldn't know about that," John said quickly. Too quickly.

"How long were you a student there?" I asked.

"Since it opened. About a year, I guess," he said warily.

"Did you like Sensei Huang?" Frank asked.

"Yeah." John sat up straight in bed. "He was great. When I started, I was just this wimpy little dweeb. But Sensei Huang taught me to stand up for myself. It changed my life."

I glanced at his biceps, which were bigger than mine. Hard to believe he'd been a "wimpy little dweeb" only a year ago. "You must have taken a lot of classes," I commented.

"It was my whole life," John said. "I made it to

52

green belt level. I took classes three days a week, and on my off days I worked out at the gym at school." He punched the sheet in frustration. "Now the doctors say I can't exert myself that much again."

"What happened?" I asked.

"I was doing my morning jog and I just collapsed," John said. "I don't really remember much. I felt dizzy, and everything went black. I woke up in the hospital."

"What did the doctors say?" Frank asked.

"They called it a heart episode." John rolled his eyes. "Whatever *that* means."

"Sounds pretty serious," I said. "You're lucky to be alive."

He snorted. "Yeah, I get to be alive but I can't do the thing I love the most. It's messed up!" He punched the sheet again.

"But you're so young, and you're in good shape. Why would you have a heart episode?" Frank asked. "Is there heart disease in your family or something?"

John scowled at us. "Why do you care? Who are you guys, anyway?"

"We're just—" I began.

"I thought you wanted to know about the Rising Phoenix. What does that have to do with my health?" he demanded.

That's what we're trying to figure out, I thought.

"Has Sensei Huang been to see you since you've been here?" Frank asked.

John winced.

"Did he come visit?" I pressed.

"Look, just get out of here," John snapped. "I have nothing to say to you guys." He turned over in bed and faced the wall, ignoring us.

Frank shrugged. "Hope you feel better soon," he told John. Then we left.

"That's one angry dude," I said as we left the hospital.

"That's also one close-mouthed dude," Frank replied. "He didn't give a single specific detail about what happened to him, or why he collapsed."

"Let's hope the other guy is more talkative," I said. "Or else we won't even know what kind of case we're working on."

"Excuse me?" I ran to catch up with a girl on her way out of Holtsville High School that afternoon. "Can you help us?"

The girl came over, smiling.

"We're looking for someone," I said. "Russell Olwell. Do you know him?"

"Not really. I know who he is, though. Everybody does, since he got mugged. They made us all sit through a self-defense and safety lecture because of him."

"Bummer," I said. "But you know, we're actually here to do a report about that mugging."

"Are you journalists or something?" she asked.

I nodded. "Think you can point me toward Russell?"

She scanned the parking lot. Tons of students were pouring out of the school and heading for their rides. "Oh, there he is!" She pointed to a short, thin guy with his arm in a cast.

"Thanks." I gave the girl a wink and headed off toward Russell.

Frank followed. "Who is that with him?" he asked, worried.

I glanced at the tall, pretty redhead with Russell. She was unlocking the passenger door of a Volkswagen Jetta for him.

"Dunno," I said. "But she's too cute to be his girlfriend."

Frank shot me a disapproving look. He thinks I'm shallow. I ignored him and put on my most charming smile. "Hi, guys," I said as we approached the Jetta. "I'm Joe and this is my brother, Frank."

The girl's eyes skipped over me, landed on Frank—and stayed there. *Uh-oh.* I knew that look.

That was the look of another girl falling for my romantically challenged brother. It was so unfair. I possessed all the flirting skills in the family, but Frank seemed to possess the chick magnet.

"Who are you?" Russell asked suspiciously.

His voice caught my attention and I stopped looking at the redhead. Instead I took in Russell's face for the first time. The dude was in bad shape. He had a black eye and a nasty bruise along his jawbone. In addition to the broken arm, there was obviously something wrong with his leg—he was struggling to get himself into the car, wincing every time he bent his knee.

"Russ, wait for me to help," the girl said. She grabbed his good arm and eased him down into the passenger seat so he didn't have to put weight on his leg. Then she turned to Frank. "Listen, my brother's hurt. I don't know what you guys want, but I really need to get him home."

Frank turned bright red. "S-sorry," he stammered.

"This won't take long," I assured her. "We just wanted to find out what happened. You're Russell's sister?"

"Samantha," she said.

"Are you telling me you didn't hear about it?" Russell asked, sounding annoyed. "I thought everyone in school knew what happened."

"We go to Bayport High," Frank replied.

"Well, I got mugged. Okay? That's the whole story." Russell reached for the door handle.

"Where?" I asked quickly. "Who did it?"

Samantha narrowed her eyes at us. "Why do you want to know?" she asked. "Why did you come all the way over here from Bayport?"

"We're, uh, detectives," Frank managed to say, not looking her in the eye. "We were hoping we could help."

"We've solved a lot of cases," I added. As if *that* would help here.

"There's nothing to solve. I got beat up," Russell said.

"He was at his martial arts school," Samantha added. "The Rising Phoenix. Some guy attacked him in the parking lot."

"Sam," Russell snapped. "Let's go."

"How long had you been studying at the Rising Phoenix?" Frank asked.

Russell just slammed the car door closed.

"Wow," I said. "Nobody wants to talk about the Rising Phoenix today."

"That's what it's about, right?" Samantha said suddenly. "It's that school!"

"What are you talking about?" Frank asked.

"My brother took classes there for a few months, and it was all he could talk about. He loved that teacher and he was so psyched. Then all of a sudden he stopped talking about it, he looked totally scared all the time, and a week later? He got attacked! Right in the school parking lot." She took a step closer to Frank. "Something bad is happening there, right?"

Frank took a step back. "We don't know."

"Well, I'm gonna find out," Samantha declared. "Enough of this guesswork. I'm going to sign up for a class and see for myself."

"Hey," I said, "we can find out what's going on there." The last thing we needed was another member of this family getting involved with Huang's school.

She looked doubtful.

"You'd stand out too much," Frank said. "Sensei Huang wouldn't trust you. You're, uh, not the type he wants there."

Samantha's eyebrows shot up. "Oh, yeah? What type is that?"

"My brother just means you're too confident and pretty," I said, ignoring Frank's embarrassed gasp. "Sensei Huang prefers to teach . . . well . . .

people like your brother. He doesn't want well-adjusted students."

She looked at me like I was nuts. Which seemed reasonable, since the whole entrance criteria seemed nuts.

She turned to Frank for confirmation. "It's true," he said. "And besides, if the school *was* somehow involved with Russell's mugging, it would be dangerous for you to be there."

"Fine. But I want you to call me if you find anything out," she said. She pulled out a pen, grabbed Frank's hand, and scribbled a number on his palm.

I thought my brother was going to pass out from the stress of actually being touched by a girl, but he managed to stay strong.

The horn honked. Russell was getting impatient.

"I better go," Samantha said, speaking to Frank as if I wasn't even there. "Good luck."

"Nice job," I said, clapping my brother on the back. "You practically got a date with her!"

"Shut up," Frank replied. "All she wants are some answers about her brother."

"He didn't seem particularly interested in helping us find any answers," I pointed out. "Weird, huh? ATAC said these two injured kids didn't have anything obvious in common. But I've noticed one similarity."

"Me too," Frank said grimly. "Neither one of them is willing to talk about what happened to them."

6
Dough-Jo

"Ready for our first karate class?" I asked Joe on Tuesday afternoon. We were at the dojo, and all geared up.

"Definitely," he said. "But really? I'm ready to find some leads on this case." He pushed open the door to the boys' locker room and led the way inside.

"Let's split up," I murmured. "We can cover more ground that way."

Joe nodded and headed for the back of the locker room to get changed. I stayed near the entrance. That way I could see whoever came in. Plus, there was a second door that led into the bathroom. And right now, that was the most interesting room in the whole Rising Phoenix school, since it was a hub of activity.

As I pulled open a locker, I noticed Billy Lee in the bathroom. He was already dressed in his *gi*. And he looked kind of freaked. I backed up and sat down on the wooden bench between the lockers, hoping to get a better view of the bathroom.

Finn Campbell stood near the sinks, arms crossed, talking to Billy.

That's the second time he's been on Billy's case since we met them, I thought. I scooted over to the end of the bench, trying to hear Finn. But it was hopeless— the sounds of other students laughing, talking, and clanging their lockers open and shut totally drowned out the conversation in the bathroom.

I moved slowly, pulling off my sneakers and socks, purposely dawdling so I could keep an eye on Billy. He was arguing now, his face red, his eyes bulging. In fact, he was yelling at Finn.

"Good for you, Billy," I murmured.

". . . not fair!" Billy's voice carried in from the bathroom. "You should have told me!"

"Man, you're slow," Joe cried, appearing next to me in his *gi*. "Hurry it up."

"Shh," I hissed. I nodded toward the bathroom. Billy had stopped arguing. He pulled a twenty-dollar bill from underneath the belt of his gi and offered it to Finn.

Finn shook his head, looking disgusted.

"What's going on?" Joe asked.

"I'm not sure. They're fighting again," I said.

"Well, I don't think a twenty is gonna cover Billy's tuition," Joe murmured.

Finn didn't seem to think so either. He leaned over and got right in Billy's face, snarling something I couldn't hear. Then he snatched the twenty and stormed out of the bathroom.

Joe jumped to his feet. "I'll see you out there, slowpoke," he said as if we were finishing a conversation we'd been having all along.

Finn jumped a little, surprised to see anyone so close to the bathroom. He shot a glance back at Billy, then pasted a smile on his face.

"The Hardys," he greeted us. "Enjoy your first class." He disappeared into the hallway. Joe followed him.

I quickly pulled on my *gi* and slammed the locker closed. Billy was still in the bathroom, splashing water on his face. I went in and pretended to be checking out my *gi* in the mirror. "Hey, Billy. What's up?" I said casually.

He glared at me. "Nothing," he snapped. He ran out before I could even react. What had happened to the nice, welcoming guy from the other day?

I headed out into the hallway just as Chet came rushing in, still in his street clothes. His backpack was stuffed so full that he had to hunch over in order to support its weight. I chuckled—Chet looked like a turtle. Had he brought every single textbook he had taken home from school with him?

"Chet, hey!" I called. "Why are you so late?"

He gave me a quick wave and ducked into Huang's office without even answering. I glanced at the clock on the wall. Class was due to start in two minutes. Why was Chet wasting time in the office? Wouldn't he get in trouble for being late?

I went to the door of the dojo and hung out there, trying to look casual. For some reason, Chet's behavior had set off an alarm bell in my head. Chet Morton is one of those guys who's always on time. He's also one of those guys who's always polite. But he'd just waved without coming over a second ago. What was the deal?

A minute later, the office door opened and Chet came out. I tried to get a look at his face, but Sensei Huang was coming out at the same time. He was saying something to Chet, but he turned so that his back was to me. He totally blocked my view of my friend. I ran my hand through my hair, frustrated. I hoped Chet wasn't in trouble for being late.

As Sensei Huang headed for the dojo, Chet vanished into the locker room. I turned away, hoping Huang wouldn't notice me watching.

But a movement in the hallway behind Huang

caught my eye. I thought I saw Liz Campbell sneak into Huang's office. I whipped my head around, but she was gone. Were my eyes playing tricks on me?

"You look worried, Frank," Huang said when he reached the dojo door. "Something wrong?"

"No, Sensei," I assured him. "I can't wait to get started."

"Good." He looked me up and down. "Why don't you come up front so you can see me better?" He took his place at the front of the room and bowed to the class. We all bowed back. I shoved my thoughts about Chet and Billy and Liz out of my head. It was time to learn some karate!

"All right, now some of you already know these basic moves," Huang called, raising his voice to be heard through the entire dojo. I glanced around. There were about twenty kids in the class. I recognized the others from our orientation group. Liz Campbell was all the way in the back, keeping to herself like last time.

"As you know, patience is of the utmost importance. Every muscle must be entirely under your control, and constant practice is the road to that level of control." Sensei Huang did his making-eye-contact thing again, looking individual students in the eye for a few seconds as he talked. "I'm going to teach the *shiko tsuki* to the new students, but I want you others to practice it right along with us. This is a basic square-stance punch."

He gazed at Joe. Joe nodded, doing his best to look insecure. That doesn't come easy to my brother.

The dojo door opened and Chet rushed in, dressed in his *gi*.

"Chet, just in time," Huang said. "Come up here and help me demonstrate the *shiko tsuki*."

Chet nodded eagerly and went to the front of the room. He positioned himself next to Huang as the sensei described the proper stance and went through the move in slow motion so we could all see exactly how it was supposed to be done.

"Chet, why don't you show them?" Huang said.

Chet dropped into a version of the square stance that Huang had described. He gave a loud "Hy-yah!" and shot his arm straight forward. Huang tumbled over backward, landing on the mat. Everybody gasped and murmured to one another, impressed.

But I couldn't believe it. Chet had barely touched the guy. I was close enough to see that my friend hadn't done anything the way Huang had showed us. Chet's feet weren't in the right position, his weight was distributed unevenly, and his punch had been slow and weak. He'd barely even covered the distance between himself and Huang.

I didn't blame Chet—he'd only been doing karate for a short time.

But why had Huang acted as if that punch had knocked him down? Why was he smiling and clapping Chet on the back?

Why was our friend such a favorite with this guy?

As soon as I got into the locker room after class, I went to find Chet.

"Hey, man, nice job in class," I told him. "I wouldn't want to have to fight you!"

Chet blushed. "Nah, Sensei Huang totally helped me," he said honestly. "I still can't really get the hang of that punch." He opened his locker and pulled out his jeans and sneakers, then his backpack.

"What's in that thing, anyway?" I asked, reaching for the strap. "You were totally weighted down before."

Chet looked panicked as I pulled the pack away from him. It swung easily through the air and bumped against my legs. I stared down at it in surprise. The pack was empty. Or at least it was light enough that it seemed empty. What had happened to all the stuff Chet was carrying?

I glanced at him and raised my eyebrows. "This pack was jammed when I saw you in the hall before class," I said.

"Um . . . I just had my *gi* in there." Chet didn't meet my eyes. He pushed his feet into his sneakers, grabbed the backpack, and headed for the door. "Listen, Frank, I gotta run. Later." He took off, still wearing his *gi*.

"Ready to go?" Joe asked, tossing his rolled-up *gi* on the bench near my locker. He took one look at my expression and knew something was wrong. "What is it?"

"Chet. He's acting weird," I said. "He came in late with his backpack all stuffed with something, and he went to talk to Huang. Just now, his pack was empty. And when I asked him about it, he bolted."

"Plus, he's getting the teacher's pet treatment from Huang and he's not even good at karate," Joe said.

"You think we should be worried?" I asked.

Joe thought about it, then shook his head. "Nah. Everybody else is all gaga over Huang too. Chet's probably just psyched someone is paying attention to him. The gym teachers at school are always kinda mean to him."

"Yeah. Maybe it's part of Huang's plan to build

up Chet's self-esteem," I agreed. A quick glance around the locker room showed me that we were alone. "Everybody's gone. Do you want to hang out and see what we can find out about Huang's background?"

"Definitely." Joe led the way to the door. "First stop, the office of Mr. Paul Huang."

"That's *Sensei* Paul Huang to you," I joked.

We'd both kept our shoes off so we could walk silently. The hall was deserted, but you never knew who might be around. We inched up to Huang's office. The door was ajar. I gave Joe a thumbs-up and reached out to push it open.

". . . a very serious situation," Huang's voice came from inside.

I snatched my hand back and shot my brother a warning look. Huang was still here!

Joe ducked down and moved underneath the big window in the office wall. Slowly, he lifted himself up until he could see inside. I held my breath. That was a risky move. If Huang happened to be facing the window, he'd see Joe for sure.

Joe stared inside for a few seconds, then dropped back down and crawled over to me.

"It's Huang and Finn," he whispered. "And Billy Lee."

Billy! Had Finn dragged their fight to Huang now too? "Is Billy upset?" I asked.

"Practically crying," Joe confirmed.

"I have to see this." I crawled over and eased myself up to the window the way Joe had. Huang sat at his desk while Finn spoke in his ear. Both looked totally serious, and Huang's eyes never left Billy's face. It was like his friendly eye contact routine in class, only this time it wasn't friendly. It was threatening.

Billy sat in the chair across from them, trembling like a scared rabbit.

When Finn stopped speaking, he straightened up and turned to Billy, arms crossed over his chest.

"I can't allow this," Huang's voice drifted out to me.

"But Sensei—" Billy began.

"What else do you have?" Huang asked.

Billy reached down into his backpack and pulled out another twenty-dollar bill. "Just this."

Huang and Finn looked at each other, and Finn shrugged.

"Fine. That will have to do," Huang said. "But next time we need the full amount, Mr. Lee."

What was this? My brain spun with possibilities. Had Billy's mother not paid tuition? Maybe Billy was taking classes without permission, and he had to scrape up the tuition money by himself? Maybe he'd gotten ripped off by the bully at school, and had his tuition money stolen?

Huang pulled a bulky brown packing envelope out of his desk and tossed it to Billy. The poor kid tried to catch it, but missed. He bent and picked it up off the floor.

"The money?" Finn said coldly.

Billy gave him the twenty. Then he bolted for the door so fast that Joe and I barely had time to get out of there. We sprinted back to the locker room and rushed inside.

"What was that all about?" Joe asked.

"I don't know," I said. "But whatever is going on here, Finn Campbell's involved."

7
California (Diner) Trail

I sat on the front steps outside school on Wednesday afternoon, my motorcycle helmet on my lap and the spare helmet next to me. We had an hour before class started at the Rising Phoenix.

"Hi, Joe," Chet called, stumbling out of the school doors while zipping up his jacket. He gave me a cheerful smile and came over.

"Hey," I said. "What did you think of Petersen's bio test today?"

"It was a killer." He rolled his eyes. "And I think Brian Conrad was trying to cheat off me."

"Figures." I laughed. "Listen, I thought you might want a ride to the Rising Phoenix. I mean, since we're going there anyway." I offered him the spare helmet.

Chet gazed longingly at it. He loves our bikes—who wouldn't? He's always trying to find excuses to borrow a motorcycle, but Frank and I never let anyone ride on their own. The bikes are far too valuable to risk—and so are the people. Still, Chet is usually pretty happy just to get a ride on the back of one.

But instead:

"Um . . . no thanks," he said.

Huh?

"But how are you gonna get to class?" I asked. "Is your mom picking you up?"

"No. I have my mountain bike." He gestured to the bike rack, where a tangle of bikes were chained up. "I'll ride."

"We can bring you back here after class to pick up your bike," I said.

Chet shuffled his feet and looked away. "That's okay. I want the exercise. I'm trying to get in shape, you know? Sensei Huang inspired me. He says you have to be strong to do your best work in karate. He encourages everybody to eat right and work out and take vitamins and stuff."

"Okay," I said. "Good for you."

"Yeah." He didn't sound convinced. "Thanks for the offer, though." He went over and began unlocking the chain from his mountain bike.

74

Frank showed up just as Chet hopped on and started pedaling away.

"I thought you were going to give Chet a ride," Frank said.

"He didn't want one."

Frank's eyes went wide. "I told you there was something strange going on with him."

"Yup." I stood up and put on my helmet. "That's why we're gonna follow him."

Sounds easy, right? But you try following a guy on a bicycle when you're on a superpowerful, completely torqued motorcycle. Our rides aren't the quietest in the world. And it's nearly impossible to go slow enough to stay behind a regular bike.

Frank and I ended up pulling over to the side of the road, letting Chet get nearly out of sight on his bicycle, and then following him at the lowest speed with our hazards on. Sometimes we even walked our bikes after him.

"I can't believe I'm saying this, but maybe supercool, standout motorcycles aren't the best vehicles for detective work," I told Frank.

"I'm going to pretend I didn't hear that," Frank replied.

Luckily, Chet wasn't the greatest cyclist in the world. He weaved a little as he rode, and he stayed totally focused on the road in front of him. He never even glanced over his shoulder to see why the noise of two motorcycles was constantly behind him.

By the time we got to Holtsville, I was sick of riding slow. Chet was obviously just going to the Rising Phoenix. "You wanna knock off and head to school?" I said.

"Not yet," Frank said. "Look."

Chet was turning—seven blocks before the turn for the Rising Phoenix. I pulled over and waited for Frank to pull up next to me. He yanked off his helmet. "Where is he going?"

I squinted after Chet, who was riding down a deserted, industrial-looking street. "Isn't this the road to the Holtsville train station?" I asked.

"I think so." Frank frowned. "But why would Chet go there?"

"Only one way to find out." I kicked the bike into gear and took off—slowly—after our friend. Frank put his helmet back on and followed me.

Sure enough, after five blocks the street came to an end in a T-intersection with the train tracks. A tiny, run-down station stood near the tracks, surrounded by a huge parking lot filled with the cars of people who commuted to work on the train. But since it was the middle of the afternoon, the place was deserted. Nobody would be back from work for another few hours.

"Where's Chet?" I asked. I couldn't see him anywhere.

"Over there." Frank pointed to a small strip mall across a side street from the station. Chet was chaining his bike to a lamppost.

"Okay, this is seriously bizarre behavior," I said.

Chet grabbed his backpack and headed over to a tiny restaurant with a neon sign that said CALIFORNIA DINER. Another neon sign was shaped like a palm tree—the only remotely Californian thing about the place. And a third sign read LUNCH SPECIALS.

"Maybe he's hungry from riding his bike so hard," Frank guessed.

But before Chet could even reach for the door handle, the glass door swung open and a tall, thin man stepped out. He spoke to Chet for a few seconds, then handed him a big, bulky package.

Chet put his backpack on the ground and struggled to get the package inside it. Finally he managed to stuff it all in. He pulled the zipper closed and looked up. The tall guy nodded and went back inside. Chet headed for his bike.

"I think we've seen enough," Frank said. "Let's get to the Rising Phoenix."

"Yeah, and keep a watch out for Chet," I added. "Showing up for karate class with a full backpack seems to be a habit for him. I think we ought to find out what's inside."

I gunned the engine and took off at top speed. It was a rush to be able to ride full-out after twenty minutes of inching along like I was on training wheels.

When we got to the Rising Phoenix, we changed quickly into our *gis*. We wanted to be sure we were ready for action by the time Chet got there. I glanced around the locker room for Billy Lee, but I didn't see him.

I went out into the hallway and hung around near the front door. Frank took up a position just inside the dojo entrance. He practiced the *shiko tsuki* punch we'd learned at the last class, but he kept his eyes on Huang's office. After a while, I noticed that Liz Campbell was also hanging around in the hallway. I glanced at her, but she looked away.

Finally it got too weird. I went over to her. "Hey, Liz," I said. "What are you up to?"

She blushed. "Oh, I was just waiting for Chet," she admitted.

I grinned. "You kinda have a thing for him, don't you?"

"I'm being stupid. He barely even says hello to me," she said.

I glanced over her shoulder. I could see through the front doors, and Chet was just pulling up on his bike, huffing and puffing with the effort. "Tell you what," I said to Liz. "When Chet comes in, just act like I'm saying something really funny. It will look like we're flirting and Chet will get jealous."

She stared at me like I had just grown a horn from my head or something.

"Trust me," I said. "I know how the romance thing works."

Chet pushed open the door and dragged himself inside, still breathing hard. Liz looked panicked, but she started to laugh loudly. So did I. Hey, it was a good cover for me—I could see everything Chet was doing, but it looked as if I was just standing there, flirting with Liz.

Chet immediately looked over at us. He seemed surprised to see me with Liz, but he quickly turncd away. He went to Huang's office and pushed open the door without even knocking.

I took Liz's elbow. "Let's walk into the dojo together," I suggested.

She laughed nervously—she probably wasn't used to guys actually touching her—and she went along with me toward the dojo. I slowed down as we passed Huang's office door.

It was standing open a little—wide enough for me to see Chet inside.

He had taken the bulky package out of his bag.

And he was giving it to Paul Huang.

8
Bad Medicine

"Okay, everybody, listen up," Huang called after the traditional bow exchange in class. "Every other class is a practice session. So that means today we're going to work with partners so you can perfect your technique. Those of you who have been here longer, you'll spend time on all the moves you've learned. Those of you who are new, you'll work on the *shiko tsuki*. So pair up with someone at your own level."

I saw Liz's face fall. She'd probably been hoping to work with Chet. "We have to be partners," I told Joe. "We need to talk."

He nodded.

"My student teacher, Marty, will be overseeing the room," Huang went on. "And I'll check in from time to time. Let's get going!"

Marty came in and bowed. We all bowed back, and I took a good look at the guy. He was gigantic! I could hardly believe his arms even fit into his *gi*. But he didn't appear to be much older than me. I wondered how he'd gotten to be the student teacher. Huang obviously trusted him—the sensei had already left the dojo.

"Pair off and start working," Marty called. "I'll be around to help individually. Call me if you have any questions."

I turned to Joe and bowed. He bowed back. "I'll go first," he said. "You block." He did the *shiko tsuki*—slowly, so he could focus on the technique.

"I saw Chet go into Huang's office, but I couldn't get a good look at what he did in there," I said quietly.

"He handed off that package from the restaurant," Joe told me. "He's obviously working as a courier for Huang. This is the second time he's done it."

"Maybe that's why Huang favors him," I commented, blocking Joe's third *shiko tsuki* move. "Because he does Huang's dirty work."

"Hang on," Joe cried. "This is Chet we're talking about. He doesn't do anyone's dirty work."

From the corner of my eye, I saw Marty turn

toward us. I quickly did the *shiko tsuki*, accompanied by a "Hy-yah!"

Joe, surprised, blocked it. "What did you do that for?" he whispered. "I thought it was my turn."

"Your voice was getting loud," I said. "Marty noticed."

Joe grimaced. "Sorry. I don't want *that* guy on our case. Dude's huge." I did the punch again and Joe blocked it. "I'm just saying that I don't think we should jump to conclusions. Chet would never get involved with a lowlife like Paul Huang," he said.

"We don't know for sure what Huang's up to," I pointed out. "And we have no idea what was in that package Chet brought him. For all we know, it was Huang's dinner!"

"You two, separate," Marty growled, coming up to us. "You're doing more talking than sparring."

Uh-oh. "Sorry," I told him, trying to sound meek.

He nodded, sizing me up. "You, work with me," he said. "You," he nodded toward Joe, "go over and work with Liz."

Joe didn't even try to hide his grin. Sure, he gets to work with a girl from the beginners' group while I get stuck with the Incredible Hulk. I sighed, bowed, and did the *shiko tsuki*. Marty blocked it the same way Joe had, but with Marty, it felt like my arm had hit a brick wall. He didn't even bend a little bit.

Marty stood up, bowed, and then did the *shiko tsuki* himself. I shot my arm up to block him, but he plowed right through it, his fist coming within half an inch of my face. I gasped and wobbled backward.

"You have to keep your stance strong," Marty coached me. "Feet planted solidly. Weight distributed evenly. Otherwise, my blow can knock you off balance."

"Yeah, I got that," I said wryly.

He cracked a smile. "Let's try again." He did the *shiko tsuki*, I focused on my balance and held my arm up to block. He hit me pretty hard, but my block held.

"Better," Marty said.

"Thanks." I rubbed my arm. It was unbelievable how strong this guy was. "You obviously know what you're doing. How long have you been studying with Sensei Huang?" I asked.

"Ten months," Marty said. "And when I started, I was as scrawny as Billy Lee over there. This place has completely changed my life."

I glanced at Billy, who was working with Chet. Billy was a pretty small guy. How could someone like that turn into someone like Marty so quickly?

"That's quite a growth spurt," I said.

Marty chuckled. "That's what my mother says. But Sensei Huang got me on a strict workout regimen, and I take classes here every day."

"Cool," I said.

"You rested enough?" Marty asked. "Let's try again."

I bowed to him, resigned. I had a feeling this would be a long, hard class.

"One of us should ask Huang for help. You know, to distract him," Joe suggested at the end of class. "And then the other one slips into his office to find out what's in the package Chet brought."

I stretched my arm across my chest and winced. Marty had totally beaten up on me—I could tell I'd be sore tomorrow. "I nominate you for the 'asking Huang for help' part," I told Joe. "I don't think I can take any more help on these karate moves."

Joe nodded. "There's Huang. Let's do it now." He moved over into the group of students surrounding the sensei. I waited until Joe had Huang involved in demonstrating the proper outside block move to counter the *shiko tsuki* punch, and then I ducked into the office.

The place was a mess—papers strewn all over

the desk, drawers opened. I hesitated. Had somebody else been looking around in here? Or was this just Huang's usual way of working? It didn't look like the office of someone who was supposed to be as calm and controlled as Huang.

I glanced around, looking for the bulky package I'd seen Chet receive at the diner near the train station. There wasn't much time.

No sign of it on Huang's desk or on the chair. I pulled open a drawer and flipped through the office supplies inside. Nothing.

My foot hit something solid under the desk. I bent to look—pay dirt! There was the package, still taped shut.

Well, that's a problem.

I used my fingernail to peel up one end of the tape. I gripped the end of it and pulled. Slowly. Slowly. I couldn't risk ripping the tape. Finally I'd pulled it all the way to one side. The package gaped open. And it wasn't full of Huang's dinner. Inside were a bunch of brown envelopes—which looked a lot like the one Huang had given Billy Lee.

I pulled one out and opened it. A small, unmarked pill bottle lay inside. The pills were just small white tablets with no markings. I frowned. If this was medicine, why wasn't it labeled?

Where was the prescription information?

I grabbed another envelope. Maybe the pills in there would be labeled.

"Hang on for a minute," Finn said. His voice sounded loud. I glanced up and saw him through the window into the hall. He stood right outside the door.

I ducked down, stuffed the envelopes back into the package, and pulled the tape back over the top, pressing down hard so it would stick.

Finn was probably just on his way to his own office, but it didn't hurt to be safe. I put the package back under Huang's desk.

"Let me just grab the class schedule," Finn added. He was still right outside.

And the doorknob began to turn. . . .

I was trapped!

Hide under the desk? That wouldn't work. What if Finn was really coming for the package? He'd know it was under the desk, and he'd see me.

I glanced around the office. There was nowhere else to hide. Finn's body was in front of the door, so he couldn't see me through the interior window.

I had no choice. I ran for the window. Quickly I yanked up the shades and pushed on the windowpane. It opened outward.

The door creaked open.

I didn't look back. I leaped up onto the windowsill, swung my feet over the edge, and dropped through the open window. I had to duck so my head didn't hit the glass.

As I fell, I heard Finn step into the office.

Did he see me?

I landed on my feet and took off, running along the side of the building until I reached a thick bush that grew about fifteen feet away. I dove under it.

Finn stuck his head out the window, looking around suspiciously. I held my breath. Finally he shrugged, shook his head, and pulled the window closed.

Made it!

I stood up and headed around the building toward the front door. But before I got to the end of the building, Liz Campbell stepped out in front of me.

"What was that all about?" she asked.

Busted!

"Uh . . . what?" I asked lamely.

"You just jumped out the window and hid in a bush," she said, raising an eyebrow. "I saw you."

"It's stupid." I shook my head, trying to look sheepish. "I was snooping around in the sensei's office. You know, looking for lesson plans or something from the advanced class."

"Why?" Liz sounded dubious.

"I just wanted to start working on more advanced moves. You know, so I could show off to Joe," I told her. "We can get pretty competitive. He bet me that he'd make it out of the beginners' class before I do."

"Huh." Liz thought about that for a moment. "So did you find anything?"

"No," I said. "I guess Sensei Huang doesn't like to write things down."

"He prefers to wing it," Liz said with a shrug. "See you later." She wandered off.

But I was worried. What did she mean, that Huang liked to wing it?

And more importantly, was she going to tell her father that I'd been snooping around in the office?

9
Suspect Behavior

"So the pills weren't labeled, and the bottles weren't labeled," I said that night. I tossed my mini-basketball through the hoop on my bedroom door. "Basically, we know nothing, and it's already Thursday."

"Not true," Frank replied. "We know that Chet has been picking up packages filled with pills from the California Diner at the train station, and we know that he's been carrying them back to Huang."

"And I guess we know that Huang has been giving those pills to Billy Lee and making him pay for them," I said.

"If he's been giving them to Billy, chances are he's been giving them to other students, too," Frank said grimly.

I shot the b-ball again. "What do you think they are?" I asked.

Frank shrugged. "If it was all legal, I doubt Huang would be sending Chet to pick them up for him. Why not just do it himself?"

"Maybe he's too busy," I suggested. "There's no way Chet would be involved in anything illegal."

But Frank shook his head. "A karate teacher taking money from students for unlabeled pills, and having another student pick them up from some random guy at a diner? It's pretty weird."

"Add that to students ending up in the hospital, and Finn obviously bullying Billy Lee, and it looks bad," I agreed. I hated to think my friend Chet would be willing to help out a lowlife like Huang. But it seemed obvious that he was. "I can't believe I'm saying this, but I think we have to consider Chet a suspect."

"You sure this is a good idea?" Frank asked me as we walked up to Billy Lee's house after school the next day. I'd tracked down his address online.

"Sure," I said. "First of all, we have to find out what Finn and Huang have been saying to him to get him so upset lately. And we know for a fact that Billy has a bottle of those pills. Maybe he can tell us what they are."

"Let's just hope he's willing to talk," Frank said.

"He was the first one to talk to us at the Rising Phoenix," I pointed out. "He's a nice guy. He'll talk." I rang the bell.

A pretty middle-aged woman answered.

"Hi. Mrs. Lee?" Frank asked. "We're friends of Billy's."

She looked surprised. "From school?" she asked.

"Uh, no, from the Rising Phoenix," I said. "The martial arts center."

"Oh, of course." Mrs. Lee held the door open for us to come in. "Billy's favorite place in the world. He never stops talking about his karate classes."

"Yeah, it's a lot of fun," I agreed. "My brother and I just started last week, but we love it so far."

"Billy made us feel really welcome," Frank put in. "He seems to have gotten a lot from his classes there."

"Oh, yes," Mrs. Lee replied. "He loves Sensei Huang. What a wonderful man—he's taken such an interest in Billy, giving him private lessons and all."

While she talked, I looked around the house. It was filled with antiques that looked pretty expensive. It didn't seem like Billy's parents would have any problem paying his tuition at the

Rising Phoenix. I had a feeling that whatever money Billy and Finn had been fighting about was money that Billy's mother knew nothing about. Was Billy buying pills from Huang without telling his mom?

"Why don't you boys go on upstairs?" Mrs. Lee said. "Billy's in his room doing homework." She craned her neck and looked at the top of the stairs. "Billy! You have guests!"

"Thanks," Frank said. He led the way up the steps. We found Billy at his desk. But he wasn't doing work. He was just sitting there, staring off into space.

"Hi, Billy," I said. "Hope you don't mind us just dropping by."

He jumped, his eyes going wide. "How did you know where I live?" he demanded. He looked pretty freaked out.

"We, uh, looked you up," Frank admitted. "We wanted to talk to you."

"*Away* from the Rising Phoenix," I added.

"Why?" Billy jumped up and closed his bedroom door. I guess he didn't want his mother to hear us.

"We noticed you arguing with Finn Campbell last week," Frank said.

"Did Finn send you?" Billy cried. His breathing was fast and he looked like he wanted to run.

"No," I said quickly. "You seemed pretty upset. We just wanted to make sure everything is okay."

"Oh." Billy frowned. "Does Finn know you're here?"

"No. Why?" Frank asked. "Would he be mad?"

"I don't know." Billy picked up his pencil and began to fidget with it.

"Billy, what's going on?" I asked. "Are you in some kind of trouble with Finn? Or with Sensei Huang?"

He shook his head, not looking at us.

"You really loved karate lessons when we first started," Frank said. "You don't seem too happy now, though."

"I'm fine," Billy said. "Look, I have a lot of homework, so . . ."

He wanted us to leave. But he still hadn't told us a single useful thing! It was time to try another tactic. "Billy, you said the sensei gave you some Chinese herbs, right?"

Billy swallowed hard. "Yeah," he muttered.

"What are they like?" Frank asked. "Like oregano or wheat germ or something that you sprinkle on your food? Or are they in pill form?"

"Yeah, they're pills," Billy said. He pulled a bottle out of his desk drawer—an unmarked bottle filled with unmarked white pills. "I take two a day."

"Sounds pretty easy," Frank said. "Do they work?"

"Yeah." But Billy didn't sound too happy about it.

"Cool. Do you think I could try one?" I asked.

Billy shoved the bottle back into his desk. "No," he said. "I mean . . . I don't think Sensei Huang would like that."

"Okay," I replied. "I guess I can just ask him for some myself."

Billy opened his mouth as if he wanted to protest. Then he closed it again. He shrugged. "I should do my homework," he said.

"Right. Thanks, Billy. See you at the next class." Frank opened the door and went out into the hall.

I took one last look at Billy. The kid seemed miserable. "You sure you're okay?" I asked.

He nodded without turning around.

As soon as we got outside, I turned to my brother. "Whatever Huang is up to, it's making a good guy like Billy turn into a total sad sack."

"I know," Frank said. "And in order to figure this out, we have to get our hands on one of those pills!"

10
The Source

After leaving Billy's, we rode over to the bike parking area in front of the Rising Phoenix. Joe was right behind me. We didn't have class that day, but we didn't want to wait until the day after to ask Huang about the pills.

"Billy said Huang offered the herbs to him," Joe murmured as we headed for the front door. "Maybe we should try doing what he did—say there's somebody picking on us. You know, get Huang to want to help us out one-on-one, then hint that we heard about his Chinese herbs."

I shook my head. "He won't buy it. I think he's suspicious of us already just because we're not as insecure as a lot of the other students. Besides, that would take too much time."

"Okay. I want to get to the bottom of this as fast as you do," Joe said. "I want to clear Chet's name."

"I hope we can," I said. The last thing I wanted was to find out Chet was deep into something illegal. But so far it seemed to be the case.

SUSPECT PROFILE

<u>Name:</u> Charles "Duke" Ducatowski

<u>Hometown:</u> Glenside, PA

<u>Physical description:</u> Age 26, 6'5", 165 lbs. Like a tall, thin string bean—made of steel. Don't be fooled by his weight. This guy is all muscle. Has a tattoo of a Chinese dragon on his forearm.

<u>Occupation:</u> Waiter at the California Diner

<u>Background:</u> Spent two years in reform school for petty theft. Learned martial arts while there.

<u>Suspicious behavior:</u> Provides the packages Chet Morton is bringing to Paul Huang.

<u>Suspected of:</u> Being a conspirator in whatever scam Paul Huang is running at the Rising Phoenix Martial Arts School.

<u>Possible motive:</u> Wants money? Being a waiter can't pay very well, especially at a hole in the wall like the California Diner.

We headed for Huang's office. But the door was closed and the lights were off. "Weird," Joe muttered. "You think he's off today?"

"Let's ask Finn," I suggested. "He's obviously involved in this whole thing—he's the one who was pressuring Billy for money."

But Finn's office was closed too. The place wasn't entirely deserted, though. We heard the familiar "Hy-yah!" sounds of people drilling moves in the dojo.

I went over and peered through the window. A small group of kids I'd never seen were sparring, doing kicks and jabs that we hadn't learned yet. "They must be from the intermediate class," I said.

"What are you guys doing here?"

I turned to see Marty, the student teacher I'd worked with the other day.

"We were looking for Sensei Huang," I replied. "Is he here?"

"Nope."

"Who's teaching this class?" Joe asked, confused.

"Nobody. It's the class I'm in, the advanced students," Marty said. "Some of us use the dojo for sparring practice on the days we don't have class."

"So there's no adult supervision?" I asked. Joe

rolled his eyes. I knew he thought I sounded like an overly worried nerd or something. But in my mind, it was irresponsible for Huang to have a bunch of teens hitting each other without a teacher around.

Marty laughed. "We're just practicing, man." Suddenly he dropped into a square fighting stance and did the *shiko tsuki* at me. Instinctively, I blocked it using the tips he'd given me the other day.

"Nice!" Marty slapped me on the back. "You guys are gonna do well here."

"We want to," Joe said. "And we heard Sensei Huang might be able to help us out. He's got some kind of Chinese herbs that bulk you up?"

Marty's smile vanished. "Who told you that?" he snapped. His face flushed with anger. "Where did you hear it?"

Whoa. I stepped away, shocked by the sudden change in attitude.

"Um, Billy Lee," Joe replied, his eyes wide. "He just mentioned he was taking these herbs and they helped him."

"We thought it sounded cool," I added lamely.

"He shouldn't have said anything about it," Marty growled. "Get out of here."

"Excuse me?" I asked. Was he throwing us out of our own karate school?

"You heard me. Get out." Marty got in my face, his fists clenched.

"Let's go, Frank." Joe grabbed my arm and pulled me toward the front door. Marty stalked over behind us, making sure we left.

Outside, I breathed a sigh of relief. "Wow. He just went ballistic in there."

"Yeah, it wasn't pretty," Joe said. "What a freak. One minute he's Mr. Nice, and the next minute he's throwing us out on our butts."

"Reminds me of John Mangione," I said. "Remember how angry he was?"

Joe nodded.

We climbed onto our bikes and kicked them into gear. "What now?" Joe asked.

"Well, we can't get pills from Huang today," I said. "Maybe we ought to check out where the pills came from to begin with."

"The diner near the train station," Joe said.

I nodded. "Let's go find Chet's source." I pulled on my helmet and took off, Joe racing after me.

I love riding. The speed, the motion of the bike, the feel of the road under your wheels . . . there's nothing like it. No matter what's going on in my life, taking a spin on the bike always calms me down.

I was in the zone when I heard Joe's voice over

101

the hum of the bikes. "Frank, check it out!"

Shaking off my motorcycle euphoria, I glanced to the right. In an alleyway about two blocks from the train station, a few guys were fighting. I slowed down to get a better look.

That was no fight—it was a mugging!

"It's two on one," I said to Joe. "We have to help."

Joe revved his bike and turned into the alley, speeding up. I did the same, gunning the engine so it made lots of noise to distract the muggers. We raced toward them, knowing we could stop on a dime the instant we reached them.

The two muggers looked up, startled by our appearance. They both wore ski masks over their faces. One of them took off immediately. The other one held his ground for a second, holding his victim by the throat against the wall of a building.

I squealed to a stop two feet away. The guy wore jeans and a black T-shirt, and I noticed a tattoo on his arm. But his face was entirely hidden by the mask.

He let go of the guy and bolted. Joe took off after him on his bike, while I jumped off to help the mugging victim.

The guy had dropped straight to the ground. I knew he must be unconscious.

I ran over, turned him onto his back, and checked to make sure he was breathing.

He wasn't.

I checked his wrist.

No pulse.

"Hang on," I told him. I tilted his head back and started to do CPR. I heard Joe roar back up on his bike, but I couldn't turn to him. I had to concentrate on saving this man's life.

"I'll call 911," Joe said, pulling out his cell phone.

After a few minutes, the guy still wasn't breathing. "There's something wrong," I gasped. "It's not working at all."

"Let me take over," Joe said.

I backed off, exhausted. Joe knelt next to the guy and kept administering CPR. I glanced around the alley. The man's briefcase had been flung against the far wall, and papers littered the ground in between. I grabbed a few and scanned them.

The letterhead on the top read, "InSight Investments."

I felt a chill run through my body. That was the company that was funding Paul Huang's karate school expansion.

Sirens filled the air. The ambulance had arrived, followed by a police car.

"Joe, see if there's a business card in his jacket,"

I said quickly. Joe shot his hand into the guy's pocket and pulled out a card just as the EMTs rushed up.

While they checked the guy out, I pulled Joe aside. "What's the card say?"

"Jarod Hamilton. Private Investigator," Joe read.

"He's a PI?" I asked. "That's not good."

"Why?"

"Because he was working for Paul Huang's financial backers," I said. "The papers from his briefcase had their letterhead."

"You think they hired him to check out Huang?" Joe asked. "Maybe they're suspicious too."

"Probably they're just checking up on their investment," I said. "Maybe they want to know everything about the Rising Phoenix before they sign up to fund a whole chain of Rising Phoenix schools."

"This guy's had it," the EMT said, shaking his head. He turned to us. "You boys did a good job, but he's not coming back."

"You mean he's dead?" I cried.

The EMT nodded. "I think his windpipe was crushed."

A police officer walked over to us. "Did you see what the muggers did to him?"

"Not really," Joe said. "We were on our bikes,

and we could see them swinging at the guy, but by the time we got close enough, they had stopped."

"One of them was holding him by the throat," I added.

"Sometimes all it takes is a sharp blow to the throat," the cop said, taking notes. "A swift kick or a jab. Can you describe the muggers?"

"They were wearing masks," Joe said. "I went after one of them on my bike, but he ran into the building over there, and I lost him."

"He had a tattoo on his forearm," I said. "A Chinese dragon."

Joe's eyebrows shot up. Clearly he hadn't seen that.

The cop nodded and wrote it all down, along with our phone numbers. "We're going to need you to fill out a police report. Can you come down to the station?"

"Sure," I said, glancing at Joe. "We'll have to check out the diner tomorrow instead."

The next day we sped to the California Diner right after school. Yesterday's murder had fanned our suspicion that this situation with Huang was serious. We had to figure out what was going on before anyone else got hurt.

There was a tiny parking lot in front with two

beat-up cars. We put both bikes in one space and headed inside.

It was a small place—ten tables, max. But the smell of fries hit my nose and immediately my stomach growled. Diner food is the best!

We grabbed a booth near the front door and glanced at the menus. I always get the same thing at diners: a cheeseburger and fries. Joe always gets a grilled cheese. Who knows why we bother looking at the menu at all?

"What can I get you boys?" the waiter asked, sounding bored.

"Cheeseburger," I replied. I glanced up at him—and kept right on staring. The waiter was the same tall, thin guy who'd given Chet the package the other day.

This was going to be easier than we'd thought.

"Grilled cheese on white," Joe said. He checked out the guy's name tag. "Duke."

The guy grunted.

"You a John Wayne fan?" Joe asked. "He was the Duke, right?"

"Right," Duke said. "But that's not where my nickname came from."

As they talked, I took a good look at the guy. He was thin, but I could see that he was pretty muscular. And on his forearm was a tattoo. A Chinese dragon tattoo.

"Where did you get that tat?" I asked. "It's really cool."

"Same place I got the nickname," he said, finally cracking a smile. "Reform school, ten years ago. I was sixteen."

Joe looked impressed. "Reform school? What did you do?"

"I stole a dirt bike," he said. "I was stupid."

"What does the tattoo have to do with calling you Duke?" I asked. "It's a Chinese dragon, isn't it?"

"Yeah, Duke doesn't sound very Chinese," Joe added.

"I was in a group there. They gave me the nickname," he said. "And we all got tattoos together."

"Was it a gang?" Joe asked.

"No, man. It was just a group of friends," he said. "The school had this martial arts class, and we all signed up. We've been best friends ever since. It got us through school, got us all straight, got us all out." He winked at me. "That's why I have the Chinese dragon tattoo. We were all into martial arts, so we liked the idea of the dragon."

"That's so weird," I said. "We just started taking martial arts classes."

"Yeah, at the Rising Phoenix school," Joe said. "Have you ever heard of it?"

"No." Duke snapped his waiter's pad closed and turned away abruptly. "Food'll be out in ten minutes," he said over his shoulder as he disappeared into the back.

"Geez. I thought we were getting along so well," Joe joked.

"We were, until you mentioned the Rising Phoenix," I said.

"Come on, it was the obvious next question," Joe said.

"It probably tipped him off that we were looking for info," I pointed out. "At least we found out what the deal is with that tattoo. Or should I say, *those* tattoos."

"A group of friends from reform school who are still involved in something underhanded," Joe said. "Sounds like a gang to me."

"So we've got Paul Huang, Duke, and the mugger from yesterday. All have the same tattoo," I said.

"Obviously Huang must've been in this reform school group with Duke," Joe said. "And with the mugger."

"Guess we know why Duke is supplying Huang with those pills," I said.

When we were done eating, Joe headed up to the ancient cash register to pay. I slapped down a generous tip for Duke—maybe he'd stop being suspicious of us if we were nice to him.

I pushed open the door and headed outside. Our class at the Rising Phoenix started in half an hour. Joe and I were hoping to convince Huang we needed his special Chinese herbs today, so we had to get there early.

My helmet was looped over the handlebars of the bike. I grabbed it and started to pull it on.

A fist slammed into the helmet, knocking it out of my hand.

A split second later, the fist pounded into my face.

11
Undercover Agent

I pushed open the door and stepped out into the sunshine. And the first thing I saw was some goon in a ski mask pounding on Frank.

"Hey!" I yelled. I raced across the parking lot and jumped the guy, tackling him to the ground.

He swung his arm sideways, hitting me in the neck with the side of his hand. I fell off him and he jumped to his feet in one move.

Frank stepped up. His lip was bleeding, but he still looked strong enough to give the guy a decent fight.

The guy's head swiveled back and forth between me and Frank. Then he turned and sprinted away.

"Guess he decided he couldn't take us both," Frank said, offering me a hand up.

"Let's go after him," I said.

"We don't have to. I know who it was," Frank told me.

"What? How?" I asked. "He was wearing a mask. Wait, was it the same guy who killed the PI?"

"No," Frank said. "It was Marty."

I pictured the huge student teacher kicking us out of the Rising Phoenix the other day. "How do you know?"

"I sparred with him," Frank said. "I recognize his moves. Too bad I didn't see it coming this time—I couldn't block." He bent to pick up his helmet.

"Wow. I thought he was just a big, angry dude," I said. "But I guess he's worse than we thought. He must be involved with Huang and Duke."

"Hey, guys," Chet said, pulling to a stop next to us on his mountain bike. "What are you doing here?"

I wasn't in the mood for any more confusion. I grabbed Chet's arm and turned him around to look at his back. His backpack was empty.

"You're here to make a pickup from Duke, aren't you?" I asked.

Chet's mouth dropped open. "Um . . ."

"We know you've been acting as a courier for Huang," Frank said. "We saw you."

"Oh. Well, then I guess you know." Chet shrugged. "I've been a courier for Sensei Huang for about a month now."

I couldn't believe it. Chet was acting as if this was no big deal.

"After Russ quit, the sensei asked me if I wanted the job," he went on.

"Russ?" I repeated. "Russell Olwell?"

"Yeah. Do you know him?"

"We met him," Frank said. "Are you saying that Russell Olwell used to be a courier for Huang?"

"Yeah. Then he dropped out of his class at the Rising Phoenix," Chet said.

"Chet, he got mugged outside the school and ended up in the hospital," I exploded. "He's still walking around with a cast on his arm!"

Chet blinked in confusion. "Are you sure? I heard he just quit."

"Yes, we're sure. We saw him!" I cried. "And we're also pretty sure that the reason he got mugged is the same reason that Marty just attacked Frank and me."

"And the same reason a man got mugged and killed yesterday," Frank continued. "Paul Huang is a dangerous guy, and he's up to something illegal."

"Chet, you're one of our best friends. How could you be involved in this?" I demanded. "How could you be working for him?"

"Because I've been investigating Huang for the past month," Chet said proudly. "I know exactly what he's up to!"

SUSPECT PROFILE

Name: Marty Cummings

Hometown: Holtsville, NJ

Physical description: Age 17; 5'10", 190 lbs. As big and beefy as a slab of meat. Straight dark hair, perpetual scowl.

Occupation: High school student; student teacher at the Rising Phoenix Martial Arts School.

Background: Used to be a scrawny kid until Paul Huang's karate lessons changed his life.

Suspicious behavior: Sudden, uncontrolled rages.

Suspected of: Being in league with Paul Huang's illegal activity; attacking Frank and Joe Hardy in the California Diner parking lot.

Possible motive: Loyalty to Paul Huang for turning his life around.

12

A New Plan of ATAC

"You know what the pills are?" I asked. Was it possible that Chet had solved our case before we had?

"What pills?" he said, staring at me blankly.

Joe sighed. "Chet, have you ever even looked inside the packages you carry for Huang?"

"No," he said. "I just come here twice a week, get the packages from Duke, and bring them back to Huang."

"Haven't you ever wondered what you're carrying?" I asked.

He shrugged. "Not really. Huang says they've known each other forever. I just figured it was some old friend thing."

"Did he tell you how they met?" Joe asked.

"Yeah. Ten years ago they took the same martial arts class—in reform school." Chet watched us anxiously, expecting us to be shocked.

"Just like we thought," I said. Joe nodded.

Chet looked disappointed. "But did you know they met Finn Campbell there too?" he asked.

"No," Joe said.

Chet pumped his fist in the air. "Finally! I know something you guys don't!"

I bit back a smile. Chet has always wanted to be a detective.

"But Finn is older than Huang and Duke," I said. "How could he have been in reform school with them?"

"He wasn't. He was the one who taught their martial arts class," Chet said.

Now *that* was interesting. I'd assumed all along that Finn was just the accountant and the office manager. It never occurred to me that he knew karate, too.

"How do you know all this stuff about Finn?" Joe asked.

Chet's cheeks turned red. "Liz told me," he murmured.

"I'm sorry, what was that?" Joe teased. "*Liz* told you? You mean you've actually spoken to a girl?"

115

"Shut up," Chet said, embarrassed. "I was trying to get information to build my case. She offered to help out."

That's why she was hanging around the other day when I climbed out the window of Huang's office, I realized. *Maybe she'd even been in there snooping before me.* The place had been a wreck, after all. Still . . .

"Hang on," I said. "Liz is Finn's daughter. Why would she help you find out any dirt on him?"

"She's worried about him," Chet replied. "She thinks Huang is a bad influence on her dad. Finn was out of work when Huang gave him this job, and now Finn thinks he owes Huang something."

"Liz thinks Huang is blackmailing Finn?" Joe asked.

"Finn doesn't seem like such a great guy to me," I said. "I saw him practically threatening Billy Lee."

Chet shrugged. "All I know is that Liz thinks he's in over his head."

"In *what* over his head?" Joe asked. "What exactly do you think is going on?"

Chet made a big show of looking around to make sure nobody was listening. Then he leaned in closer to us. "Huang's a fraud," he whispered.

"He's scamming the students for money?" I asked.

"Is he embezzling funds from the Rising Phoenix?" Joe asked.

Chet frowned. "No." He paused for a moment, for dramatic effect, and then revealed, "He's not a black belt."

I glanced at Joe. He looked as confused as I felt. "Huh?" he said.

"I asked Duke about Huang and his martial arts background," Chet said. "They both took classes when they were in reform school. And Duke kept taking classes afterward, but Huang didn't."

"And . . . ?" I just didn't see where he was going with this.

"And he claims to be a master karate teacher," Chet cried. "But he's not even a black belt!"

"So what?" Joe asked.

"So kids are paying to take lessons from a black belt," Chet said, speaking slowly as if that would make it easier for Joe to understand. "He's lying to them. They're not getting what they paid for."

"Okay," Joe said. "But what does that have to do with the pills that Huang is giving Billy Lee?"

"Or with those two kids who ended up in the hospital?" I added.

"Or the private investigator who got killed yesterday?" Joe asked.

Chet looked from me to Joe and back again.

"I—I don't know what you guys are talking about," he said.

"Those packages you've been carrying are filled with little white pills in unlabeled bottles," I told him. "Huang gives them to Billy—and probably a lot of other students. And it seems like he expects students to pay for them."

"Plus, Russell got mugged and another kid collapsed. And a guy with the same tattoo as Huang murdered a PI from InSight Investments in an alley about two blocks from here," Joe added.

Chet's face fell. "So it's not just about Huang lying to students?" he asked.

"No. We think it's about the pills that you've been transporting," I said.

Chet banged his hand on the seat of his bike. "I can't believe it! I'm the worst detective of all time. I never even thought about the packages. I just figured that acting as his courier was a good way to get Huang to trust me."

"That's a great idea," Joe said quickly. "You wanted him to trust you and be relaxed around you. That way he'd let down his guard and you could get the dirt on him."

"Classic detective strategy," I agreed.

But Chet wasn't having it. "You two have been here for a week and you already know more about what's going on than I do. I didn't solve the case, did I?"

"No," I admitted. "But you can be a huge part of helping *us* solve it."

"I can?" he asked hopefully.

"Absolutely. But it might be dangerous," Joe told him.

"I don't care," Chet said. "I can handle it. What's my mission?"

"Simple. Just go into the diner and get the package from Duke like you always do," I said. "Act normal. Then, after you have the pills, you'll meet us at the Rising Phoenix. We'll take one of the pill bottles so we can send it to be tested and find out what the pills are."

"Then you give the rest of the package to Huang like you always do," Joe put in. "You'll have to act as if everything is normal so Huang doesn't suspect anything."

"Can you handle that?" I asked.

"Definitely." Chet grinned. "Awesome!"

I smiled back at him. Chet was a great guy. I was beyond relieved that he wasn't involved in Huang's illegal activities—at least not on purpose. "It *is* awesome," I agreed. "We're psyched to have another detective on our team."

13
Herbal Overload

"Do you think we should be worried about Chet?" Frank asked over the helmet mikes as we rode to the Rising Phoenix. "What if Duke saw him talking to us?"

"I was watching the diner door," I replied. "Duke didn't show. I'm sure he wasn't watching."

"But still, I don't want to put Chet in danger."

"He can handle it," I told my brother. "Chet has been waiting for this chance his whole life. He'll pull it off."

When we roared up to the Rising Phoenix, I was surprised to see a tall, pretty, red-haired girl pacing up and down on the walkway in front.

"Hey, Frank, it's Samantha Olwell," I said. "Looks like she tracked you down."

He didn't answer, but I knew he was panicking. A girl, oooh, scary!

We parked the bikes and headed for the entrance.

"Frank!" Samantha rushed over. Ignoring me, of course.

"Hi, Samantha," I said.

"Oh, hey, Joe." She barely even looked at me. "I heard about that killing yesterday. The news report listed you two as witnesses. Are you okay?"

Frank nodded without saying a word. As usual, I was going to have to do his flirting for him. "We're fine," I assured her. "Although it was pretty hairy for a while there. Frank had to bust up the mugging with his motorcycle. He did CPR on the poor guy and everything. But it was too late. There was just nothing we could do."

Samantha bit her lip, still gazing at Frank. "That's awful. You must have been so upset."

"Yeah. He was," I said, shooting Frank a look that clearly said to start talking.

He cleared his throat. "How's your brother feeling?" he asked.

"A little better, physically. But I still can't get him to tell me what happened, not in any detail," Samantha said. "That's why I'm here. When I read about you two and that murder, I thought there must be some connection to the Rising Phoenix case you're working on."

Smart.

"Looks like there is a connection," I said. "Frank will tell you all about it."

Frank shot me a look of death, but I ignored him. "See you in class," I said. I gave him a little wave and headed for the door.

Liz and a few of the other kids from class were already warming up in the dojo. I nodded hello to them and pushed open the locker room door. I went straight to the back corner where I'd been changing before every class.

Marty was there.

And he was whaling on Billy Lee!

"Hy-yah!" Marty yelled, swinging his fist at Billy's chest. Billy tried to block the blow, but Marty was about ten times stronger than him. The force of the punch threw Billy sideways into the lockers.

"Stop!" I cried. I ran full force at Marty. He spun around quickly and began to swing. But I didn't bother with karate. I hurled my backpack at his head. There wasn't much in it, so I knew it wouldn't hurt him. But it was a good distraction.

Instinctively, Marty ducked.

I took advantage of his confusion to grab his arm. I twisted it around behind his back and pinned him up against the lockers. If he moved too far, I could break his arm.

"What's going on, Marty?" I demanded. "Picking on a kid half your size?"

"No," he snapped, gasping as I pulled on his arm. "We were just practicing a move for class. Right, Billy?"

I looked at Billy. He was holding his side where Marty had hit him, and his face was pale. But he just nodded.

"That's the truth?" I asked doubtfully. "Seriously, Billy?"

"Yeah. We were practicing." Billy wouldn't look me in the eye. "I should get to class." He scurried out of the locker room.

"You gonna let me go, Hardy?" Marty demanded.

Reluctantly, I released his arm and stepped away. I knew this was the second time today I'd fought him. But Marty obviously didn't think I was aware that he had jumped my brother at the diner.

He sneered at me and walked away.

I quickly changed into my *gi* and went out into the hallway. Frank was still outside talking to Samantha. I pushed open the door and stepped outside just as Chet came puffing up on his bike, riding hard.

"You're cutting it close," I said. "Class starts in about thirty seconds."

Frank pulled Chet to the side so they couldn't be seen from inside. He peeled the tape off the top of the package in Chet's backpack. Reaching inside, he took out a brown envelope with a pill bottle inside.

"I'll take this to Dad and get it tested. We need to know what these pills are," he said as I reapplied the tape to the package. We just had to hope that Huang didn't bother to count the envelopes inside—at least not until after class.

"Our father is a retired cop," I told Samantha. "He still has friends on the force who can do the lab work for him." Our dad was also a founding member of ATAC, and once he found out this was for an ATAC mission, he'd get the pills tested right away. But we couldn't tell Samantha—or Chet—about that.

"If you take the pills to him right now, you'll miss class," Chet pointed out.

"I know. But what choice do we have?" Frank said.

"Don't worry. Chet and I will keep an eye on things here," I told him. Chet beamed at me. I knew he loved to be included.

"I'll wait until you get back," Samantha said. "I want to know what's in those pills."

"Huang's coming," Chet cried. "Get out of here, Frank!"

I grabbed Chet's arm and hurried him toward the front door. We got there just as Huang reached the door from the inside. He frowned at us as we stepped into the Rising Phoenix.

"Where have you two been?" he asked. "Chet, I've been waiting for you."

"Sorry, Sensei," I answered for him. "We were all just talking." I gestured toward Chet and Samantha. Frank must've taken off already, because he was nowhere in sight.

Huang glanced at Samantha, then shook his head. "You need to concentrate. You're late for class," he said. "Talk to your girlfriends on your own time. Let's go."

He led the way back to the dojo, then hesitated. "Chet, I need to see you in my office for a moment. Joe, why don't you head on in."

I nodded and went into the dojo. I knew Chet was handing over the package right that second. Would Huang count the envelopes inside? Would he find out we'd stolen one?

For the first half of the class, I watched Huang

carefully, trying to figure out if he was angry or worried or upset. He was hard to read because he always seemed so calm. I was so distracted by thoughts of the case that I barely even paid attention to the *age uke* blocking move he was teaching us.

Before I knew it, it was time to break into partners and practice the new move.

We were supposed to stick with partners at our exact level, so I hurried over to Liz. I was glad when I saw Chet partner up with Billy again—that seemed to be their routine in every class.

"Liz, can you help me?" I murmured as we began punching and blocking. "I need to talk to Billy. It's about the, uh, case Chet is working on."

Liz's eyebrows shot up in surprise. "You know about that?"

"Yeah. Think you and I can switch partners with them?" I asked.

She glanced at Huang. He was busy working with two of the other new students in class. "Okay. Let's go." Liz began to slowly move toward Chet and Billy. Every time she punched, she managed to move another few feet. In a couple of minutes, we were standing right next to Chet and Billy.

"Chet," she said. "Can you help me? I can't get this punch right."

Chet did his insta-blush. You'd think he would

be used to talking to Liz by now, but apparently he wasn't. "We're not supposed to—"

"It's okay," I cut him off. I stared at him meaningfully, mentally urging him to go along.

"Uh . . . all right." Chet turned to face Liz, leaving me to take his place opposite Billy.

"Sorry, man," I whispered. "I think Liz and Chet have a thing going on. Can't argue with that, huh?"

Billy nodded, but I could tell he was less than thrilled to be working with me.

I did the *shiko tsuki*, and he blocked it immediately. When he was concentrating, he was actually stronger than he looked.

"That was a good block," I said.

"Thanks. I'm getting better."

"You're still no match for Marty, though," I pointed out. "Why were you practicing with him, anyway?"

Billy looked annoyed. "Because he's the student teacher."

"Is it normal to practice in the locker room like that?" I pressed.

"What is it with you?" Billy snapped. "Why are you and your brother always asking questions? It's *your* fault Marty was hitting me like that!"

He kicked, catching me off guard. I went down.

"Wow," I said, climbing back to my feet. "Guess you got me back."

Billy winced. "Sorry. I didn't follow the proper form. You weren't ready."

"It's okay. I can see you're mad at me," I told him. "I just don't understand why. How is it my fault you were fighting with Marty?"

He glanced around to make sure Marty wasn't in earshot. "You and Frank told him that I said I was taking Sensei Huang's Chinese herbs," Billy murmured. "It's supposed to be a secret. Sensei Huang doesn't want everybody knowing about it. Marty was furious."

"Why is it a secret?" I asked. "What's wrong with taking an herbal supplement?"

"I'm not sure." Billy looked miserable. "Sensei Huang has gotten really weird about it lately."

"I don't think this is going to work," Huang interrupted us. "You two are at very different levels of expertise."

Billy's eyes went wide with panic. I felt pretty freaked myself. How much of our conversation had Huang overheard?

"Joe, your form is sloppy. Go over to the mirror and work on the *age uke* by yourself until you have more control of it." Huang's tone of voice didn't leave any room for argument. I bowed to him and turned away, my face flaming. I saw Chet and Liz watching us, concerned.

"Don't worry, Billy, I'll be your sparring partner for now," Huang added as I walked away.

I tried to concentrate on the blocking move, studying my body in the mirror. Start from a balanced stance, knees slightly bent. Keep your weight centered, raise the arm, and move it in a smooth arc. . . . I did it over and over. But my eyes kept wandering to Billy and Huang. I watched in the mirror as Billy did a kick I hadn't learned yet in combination with the *shiko tsuki* punch. Huang blocked him.

They didn't seem to be saying anything to each other. Was that a good sign or a bad one? It didn't seem possible that Huang had separated us just because we were at different levels. He must suspect that we were on to him.

I kept my eyes fixed on their reflection in the mirror as I slowly went through the *age uke* move one more time.

Huang bowed to Billy. Billy bowed back. Then Huang leaped up and kicked, his leg moving at lightning speed. I saw Billy's shoulder snap back. He went down, landing on the mat.

He didn't get up.

I whirled around and ran toward him before I

even realized what I was doing. Luckily, Chet, Liz, and a few other kids were running over too.

"Billy!" I cried. "Are you okay?"

He was curled into a fetal position, his mouth open and gasping for air.

"He got the wind knocked out of him," Huang said. "Everybody, back up. Give him some air." He took Billy's arm and helped him to his feet. "I'm going to take Billy into my office to let him recover. Marty, take over, please."

He started toward the door, Billy shuffling along beside him, still gulping in air.

I moved to take Billy's other arm, but Marty stepped in front of me. "You don't have to worry about Billy," he said. "Sensei Huang will take care of him."

His message was clear—I wasn't going anywhere near Huang's office while Billy was in there. But why?

What was really about to happen in that office?

14
Master of Lies

"What are you doing home?" Aunt Trudy asked when I walked in the door. "Aren't you supposed to be at karate class?"

"Hy-yah!" Playback squawked. "Hy-yah!"

"Yes, Aunt Trudy," I said quickly. "But I forgot my *gi*. Can't do karate in jeans." I gave her a wink and raced for the stairs. I took them two at a time, then hurried down the hall and burst into my father's office.

"Dad, I need help!" I cried.

He took one look at me and closed the door. "What's going on?"

"It's for our ATAC mission," I told him. I pulled the unmarked bottle of pills out of my pocket. "We need to know what these things are, stat."

131

Dad's forehead creased with worry. "Are you boys in any danger?" he asked. "Between that killing yesterday and now—"

"Dad, don't worry," I interrupted. "We can take care of ourselves. You know that."

"Hmph," he said.

"Listen, I gotta get back to the Rising Phoenix," I said. "I don't want to leave Joe and Chet alone."

"*Chet?*" Now Dad really looked worried.

"He's not *too* involved," I assured him. "I mean, he thought he was, but . . ."

"I don't want to hear about it," Dad said, shaking his head. "You make sure he gets *un*-involved, right away."

"We will." As I left the room, he was already on the phone to ATAC, setting up lab time to test the pills.

I barreled down the stairs and headed for the door.

"Where is your *gi*?" Aunt Trudy cried from the kitchen. She gazed at me as if I'd lost my mind.

"Oh. Uh . . . I guess I didn't leave it at home after all," I said. "I must have left it in my locker at school."

"Honestly, Frank, that sounds more like something your brother would do," Aunt Trudy said. "Are you feeling okay?"

"I'm fine, Aunt Trudy," I promised her. "But I have to run." I gave her a kiss on the cheek and bolted.

By the time I got back to the Rising Phoenix, class was half over. I just hoped Joe was okay in there. I pulled my motorcycle in next to his.

Samantha was still hanging out in the parking lot. She rushed over, her face filled with worry. "What happened?" she asked. "What are those pills? What is this all about?"

"Samantha, it's too soon to know," I told her. "The pills are being tested right now. You should go home and wait. I'll call you when we find anything out."

"Oh, no," she said. "My brother's entire personality was changed by this place, and I intend to find out why. You guys don't have any right to keep me out of the loop."

"Okay, but I need to get inside," I insisted. "Joe and Chet could be in danger, for all I know. We think Huang suspects that we're, uh, snooping around."

Her eyes narrowed. "Why do you think that?"

"Because the student teacher attacked me earlier this afternoon," I blurted out. "Now, please, go home. I don't want you to get hurt."

"Are you kidding me?" Samantha cried. "I'm

absolutely not going anywhere now. You could be in trouble!"

"Fine. Stay. But I'm going inside." I couldn't argue anymore. As long as she didn't go near Huang or Marty, she'd probably be safe. They didn't know she was Russell's sister, so they wouldn't pay any attention to her.

I pulled open the front door and took two steps down the hallway.

Huang was dragging Billy into his office. I saw the kid's frightened face for a split second, and then Huang slammed the door shut behind them.

Uh-oh.

I turned around and went right back out the door.

"What are you doing?" Samantha asked.

"Huang's got Billy Lee in his office," I said. "Something's going down."

"So why are you back out here?"

"I happen to know where the window of Huang's office is. We can listen in to his conversation from there." I led the way around the back of the building and down to the window I'd climbed out of a few days ago.

It was open a few inches. Perfect! We'd be able to hear everything. I ducked down below the window so they couldn't see me. Samantha did the same.

". . . gone too far," a voice said. "You're cut off."

"Is that Huang?" Samantha whispered, putting her lips right up to my ear.

I shook my head. "It sounds like Finn Campbell," I told her. "He's the bookkeeper."

"What do you mean?" Billy asked, his voice thin and scared.

"We're not going to give you any more," Huang replied. "You haven't been paying, so you don't get any more pills."

"But I need them!" Billy said loudly. Not exactly frightened anymore—more like desperate. "I can already lift twice as much weight when I work out, and I've only been taking the herbs for two weeks. You can't cut me off!"

I felt as if someone had just smacked me in the head. Why hadn't I seen it sooner?

"Steroids," Samantha whispered in my ear.

I nodded. That's what the pills were. I didn't need a lab test to confirm it; Billy's description was enough. Herbs to help him "bulk up"? More like illegal steroids that enabled him to lift more weight and put on muscle fast.

"You don't have to stop taking the herbs," Finn said. "But you do have to start paying for them. For real, not just a twenty here and there. The pills are fifty dollars a week."

I glanced at Samantha. Her eyes were wide. Fifty bucks a week? That was pretty steep. Who could afford that? It's not like Billy had time for a job in addition to school and all the karate classes he was taking. He was probably too young to work, anyway.

"But I don't have that much money," he said, echoing my thoughts.

"Well, you'll have to find it somehow," Finn told him.

"If you don't pay up, I'm afraid we'll have to talk to your mother," Huang added in that calm monotone of his. "And I doubt she'll be very happy to hear that you've been taking steroids. They're illegal, you know. You're breaking the law."

"But . . . but you said they were just herbs. . . ." Billy's voice cracked. It sounded like he was crying.

My head spun. Finally I got it.

Billy had been totally up front with us—he thought he was taking Chinese herbs because that's what Huang had told him.

"Huang gets kids hooked on steroids," I whispered into Samantha's ear. "He says they're harmless herbs. Then, once the kids get used to taking them and like the results, he makes them pay."

"Not just that. He's blackmailing this boy," Samantha whispered back. "If he doesn't pay,

Huang will tell his mother he's taking illegal drugs. He'll get in huge trouble—but he didn't even know he was doing anything wrong!"

I nodded. Huang was nothing more than a drug dealer, preying on kids who were weak and lacked self-confidence. What a lowlife.

It was time to call the cops. I reached for my cell phone—

—and someone tackled me from behind.

I fell to the ground, my face in the dirt. He was on top of me, pinning me down. I couldn't move!

"Hey!" Samantha yelped. She balled her hand into a fist and swung at him, managing to land a punch before his hand shot out and grabbed her by the throat. He shoved her back into the wall, her head smashing against the brick.

I recognized that move. It was how the mugger had killed that private investigator. This was the same guy!

Samantha's eyes rolled up in her head and she dropped to the ground. Had he killed her?

I crawled over and grabbed her wrist, feeling for a pulse.

She was alive.

"You're next," the guy growled.

I jumped to my feet and turned to face him.

It was Duke.

15
Rumble in the Dojo

"I'm going after Billy," I told Marty. "You can't stop me."

The other students had all stopped sparring by now. They were watching us, totally confused.

"You're not going anywhere, Hardy," Marty growled. "What happens between Sensei Huang and that little twerp is none of your business."

"What do you mean?" I demanded. "What's going to happen between them? What is Huang gonna do to Billy?"

"To Billy?" Liz cried. "What do you mean?"

"Huang's a bad guy," I said, turning to face her. I raised my voice so the entire class could hear me. "He kicked Billy too hard on purpose. I think he may be hurting him right now."

"You're insane," Marty said.

"Fine. Then let me go see what's going on in the office." I moved for the door.

Marty did a *shiko tsuki*. Luckily, I was expecting it. I ducked under the blow and turned on him with a punch of my own.

I connected, hitting hard. He barely even flinched. The guy was pure muscle—it was like hitting a cinderblock.

He attacked, the blows coming fast. Punches combined with kicks and other blocking moves I hadn't even learned yet. I just kept blocking and ducking. I couldn't even think about getting to the door yet—it took everything I had just to keep Marty from seriously hurting me.

Chaos broke out around us. One or two of the kids tried to grab Marty and pull him back, but he shook them off like drops of water.

I heard people shouting, but I tuned them out. I had to focus on Marty. His eyes never left my face, and they were filled with rage. He wasn't about to stop until he'd pounded me into the ground.

"Chet, call the cops!" I yelled.

Marty flew at me, fists moving so fast I could barely see them.

"Why are you doing this?" I gasped as I tried to block his blows. "Huang's a loser."

"It's my job," Marty grunted.

"He pays you to be a bully?" I cried. "Why don't you just work at McDonald's and save yourself the trouble?"

"Sensei Huang is a great man," Marty bellowed, stopping for a moment. "He changed my life! Before he gave me those herbs I was a total weakling. I got beat up every day. Now look at me!"

"Yeah, now you're the jerk beating other people up," I snapped.

"I don't care," he yelled. "I'm not going back to being a wimp."

Something clicked in my brain. "You're not working for money," I said. "You do what Huang says and he gives you those pills."

"I need them," Marty growled. "I can't afford to pay, so I work for them. There was no problem until you showed up. I knew you and your brother weren't really here for classes. Why did you have to mess everything up?"

He charged me again, spinning and kicking. I ducked to one side, then the other. But I was already winded. He was way too strong and way too fast.

"You're out of your mind," I grunted. "Huang's got you acting like a criminal."

"I don't care," Marty said. "I'll do whatever it takes."

"Including mugging Russell Olwell a month ago?" I asked. "And attacking my brother today?"

"You mugged Russ?" one of the other kids cried.

"He was a snitch," Marty said with a sneer. "He found out what he was carrying and he threatened to rat on Huang. He deserved it."

"You put him in the hospital," I cried. "You're a total thug."

Two of the other kids grabbed Marty's arms and tried to pull him away again. The rest of the class was just sort of huddled in the back of the room. They looked seriously freaked. No one knew what to do.

Marty roared like an animal and brought his arms together fast—slamming the two kids into each other. They both fell.

He stepped over them, coming for me, his face twisted with rage. "I will not let you ruin this for me," he snarled. "I will not go back to being a loser!"

He jumped into the air, getting ready to kick. His foot came at my chest.

I didn't know how to block it. I felt too tired to

move. He was going to get me this time. I waited for the blow.

And that's when Marty's leg dropped. His jaw went slack. And he crumpled to the ground like a rag doll, unconscious.

16
Outnumbered

Duke's fists flew at my head. I ducked and covered my face, trying to punch him in the stomach or the chest. Trying to avoid the blows.

But he was an expert fighter. He hit me again and again, his hands pummeling my face and shoulders.

"Joe!" I yelled as loud as I could. "Get out here! Joe!"

The window swung open. Was it my brother coming to help?

No. It was Huang. He peered out at Duke and me. "What's going on?" he snapped.

"This jerk has been snooping around," Duke told him. "He was listening under your window."

I was too exhausted from fighting to even try to get away. I just concentrated on catching my breath so I'd be strong enough to defend myself.

"I'll be right there," Huang said grimly. He turned and ran for his office door. He yanked it open—

—and Joe's fist smashed into his face.

I grinned. My brother was right on the other side of Huang's door. He didn't wait for Huang to recover. He punched him again.

"You better hope the cops get here soon, Huang," Joe snapped. "Marty just collapsed."

"It's from steroids," I yelled. "Right, Huang? You give kids steroids so they get big and muscular like Marty. But they're unhealthy. They ruin your liver and weaken your heart. That's why John Mangione collapsed when he was jogging. That's why Marty just collapsed now. You're lucky you haven't killed anyone yet."

"That's enough out of you," Duke growled. He leaped into the air and aimed a kick at my head. I jumped to the side just in time.

From the corner of my eye, I saw Huang jump at Joe, fists flying.

Before Duke could attack again, I grabbed the windowsill and heaved myself up. I swung over and landed inside Huang's office. The sensei was an expert fighter, but together Joe and I should be able to take him.

Somebody kicked me in the side.

I staggered into Huang's office chair and turned to see Finn in a fighting stance. "I should never have let you two into the school," he muttered.

My whole body went cold. I'd forgotten Finn was in here. He was the one who'd taught Huang and Duke how to fight—he was probably better than both of them!

While I was staring at Finn, Duke leaped over the windowsill like I had. He charged me, karate chops coming fast and furious.

Forget about trying to fight these guys with karate! There was no way I could beat them like that. I grabbed the back of the office chair and spun it around, then shoved with all my strength, pushing it into Duke's stomach. The back of the chair caught him right under his rib cage and he fell back with an "Oof!"

Finn jumped over the desk and hit me with a one-two chop. I stumbled backward, pain buzzing through my abdomen. Over his shoulder, I saw Joe get up and grab the door frame. He swung himself through the air and kicked Huang in the head with both feet. The sensei staggered backward but didn't fall.

By the time my brother landed back on the floor, Huang was going for him again.

Finn dropped into a fighting stance and started to swing at me.

"Dad!" Liz shrieked from the doorway.

Everybody stopped fighting and turned to look at her.

She was staring at the mayhem with a shocked expression on her face. "What are you doing?" she cried. "You can't fight with kids. You're a black belt. You could kill them!"

"That's the idea, girlie," Duke growled. He jumped at me, arm out for my throat. He'd crushed the PI's windpipe. He could do the same to me.

I ducked under his arm and slammed my head into his stomach, driving him back against a filing cabinet.

"You're a filthy murderer," I yelled at him. "You're going away for life."

"Not if you aren't around to testify," he sneered. He shot one finger out and drilled it into a point just below my shoulder blade. My muscles went slack, and I stumbled backward.

Liz ran into the office, screaming. She leaped up and kicked Duke in the side, then spun around and hit him with a one-two chop.

Part of my brain realized that she knew a lot

146

more karate than she'd let on. The other part of my brain was just trying to force my body to start working again. Duke must have hit some kind of pressure point and incapacitated me.

"Hy-yah!" Huang yelled, kicking at Joe. My brother went down.

Duke shot his arm up and blocked Liz's blows with one hand. His other hand chopped her in the neck. Her head snapped to the side.

"No!" Finn bellowed. He flew across the room and yanked his daughter out of the way.

"She's a liability," Duke snarled. "We have to get rid of her."

"She's my daughter, you Neanderthal," Finn said, his voice calm and cold. "Touch her again and I'll kill you."

"You're in too deep, Campbell," Huang said from the other side of the office. I couldn't see Joe. He hadn't gotten up again. Was he unconscious? Worse? "These kids can send us to jail. We've got to get rid of them."

Liz gasped. "Daddy?"

"No," Finn said. "I've let you drag me into enough trouble, Huang. This ends. Now."

"Yes it does," said a new voice.

My father stood in the office doorway, two cops behind him.

Duke spun toward the open window, but another police officer stood outside, blocking it.

"Interesting pills you've been giving to the kids at your school, Huang," Dad said. "The lab tests show they're illegal steroids. That makes you a drug dealer. Giving drugs to minors. You're going away for a long, long time."

Dad leaned down and helped Joe to his feet. My brother looked pretty beaten up, but he was alive. Relief rushed through my body. We'd made it!

17

Three Great Detectives

"Shouldn't you put a steak on that or something?" Chet asked me the following Monday at lunch. He squinted at the green and purple bruise on my cheek.

"Shockingly, the cafeteria wasn't offering raw steak for lunch today," I joked. "But really, it looks worse than it feels."

"Your aunt must be freaking out," he said. "I know she hates it when you and Frank go out solving crimes."

"Yeah. We told her it was just a rough day in karate class," I said. "So listen, my father found out more about Huang's background. Turns out you were right."

"About what?" Chet asked.

"He isn't a black belt. The highest level he ever achieved was brown belt—just before black." Which still made him a pretty lethal fighter, as my aching body could prove.

"Are you serious?" Chet cried happily. "So I was right! He *was* scamming students!"

"Yup, you were right," I said. "You're a pretty good detective after all."

Frank came over and sat down at the table, sticking his cell phone back into his pocket. "That was Dad," he said. "He had an update on Samantha and Marty. Samantha's fine—they checked her out last night and sent her home. Marty is still in the hospital, but he's doing okay. The doctors say he had a heart episode just like John Mangione. The heavy steroid use weakened their heart muscles, which can lead to collapse during times of exertion."

"Like when John was jogging," I said. "And when Marty was fighting me."

Frank nodded. "There are a lot of side effects. The way Marty would fly into rages—that was caused by the steroids."

"John Mangione was pretty angry when we met him too," I said.

"I can't believe this was going on and I didn't even know it," Chet grumbled.

"Nobody knew it," Frank told him. "The police think almost half of Huang's students had started taking steroids and they all thought they were taking harmless Chinese herbs."

"Huang and Duke will be facing some pretty serious charges," I said. "Finn, too, I guess. He was involved in extorting money from the students."

"He'll get a lesser sentence," Chet replied. "He's cooperating with the police—he's going to testify against Huang and Duke, and he can name a few other guys who were involved too. That whole group from the reform school has been working together, getting the illegal drugs, transporting them, mugging and killing that PI. All kinds of things. Finn knows them all because he was their teacher way back when. But he wasn't involved in anything illegal until Huang gave him the job at the Rising Phoenix a year ago."

"You sure know a lot about Finn Campbell." I waggled my eyebrows at him. "Been talking to Liz? Hmmm?"

Chet didn't even blush. "Yeah. She's pretty upset about her dad. But I think she'll be okay."

"So is she your girlfriend now?" Frank asked, impressed.

"Nah. We're just hanging out," Chet said casually.

"Huang pretended he wanted to help kids gain more self-confidence," I said. "Looks like it actually worked on you."

Chet grinned. "I don't think he planned it this way. I'm kind of bummed, though. I really wanted to learn karate."

"Me too," Frank said.

"I know what you mean," I told them. "After seeing those guys in action, I want to learn to fight like that too."

Frank shot me a look, and I knew what he meant: The moves we learned would come in handy for our future ATAC missions.

"So what do you say, guys?" I asked. "Want to take some karate lessons?"

"We already have our *gis*," Frank replied.

"Okay." I held out my hand, knuckles facing them. My brother and Chet bumped fists with me. "It's a plan."